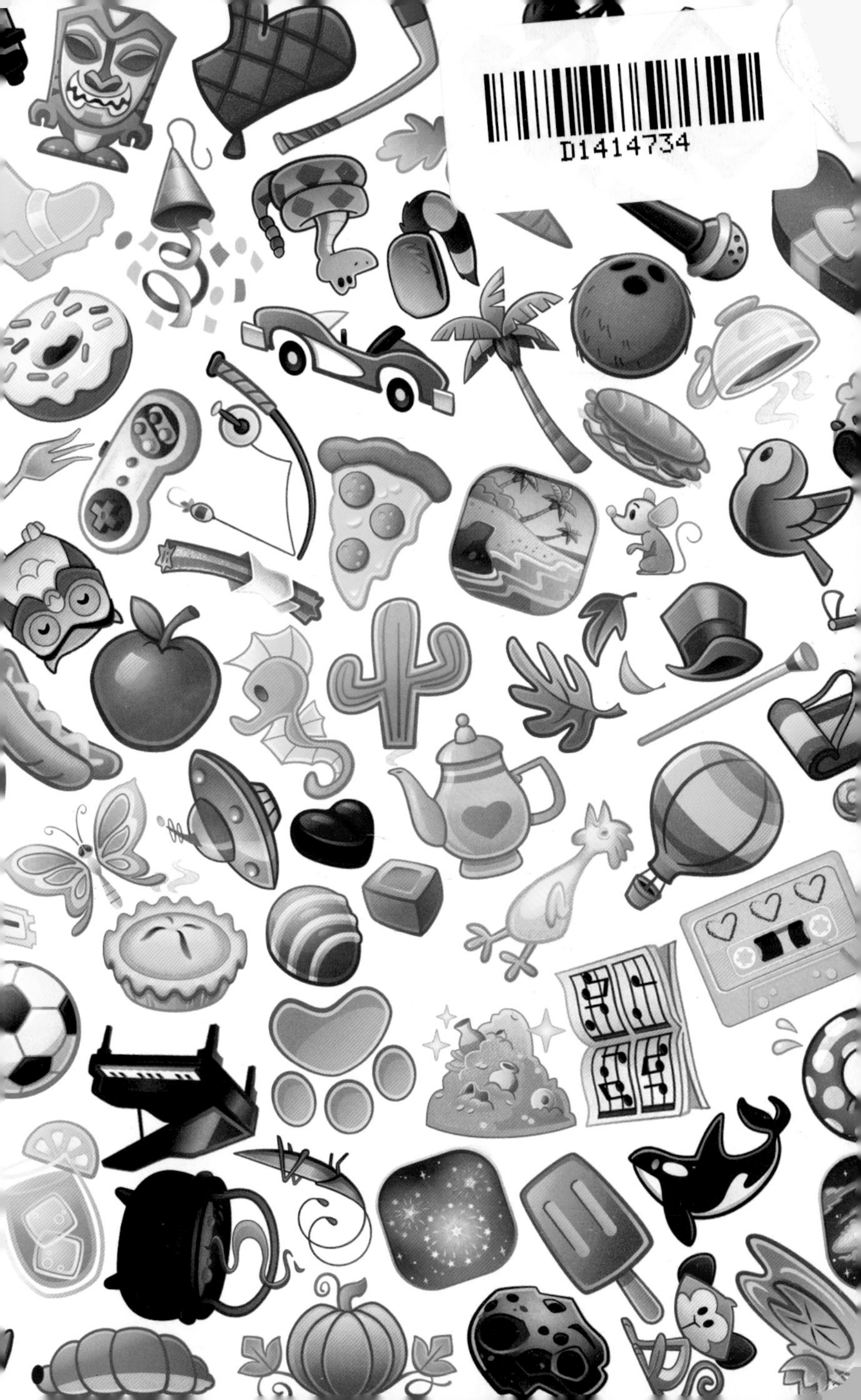

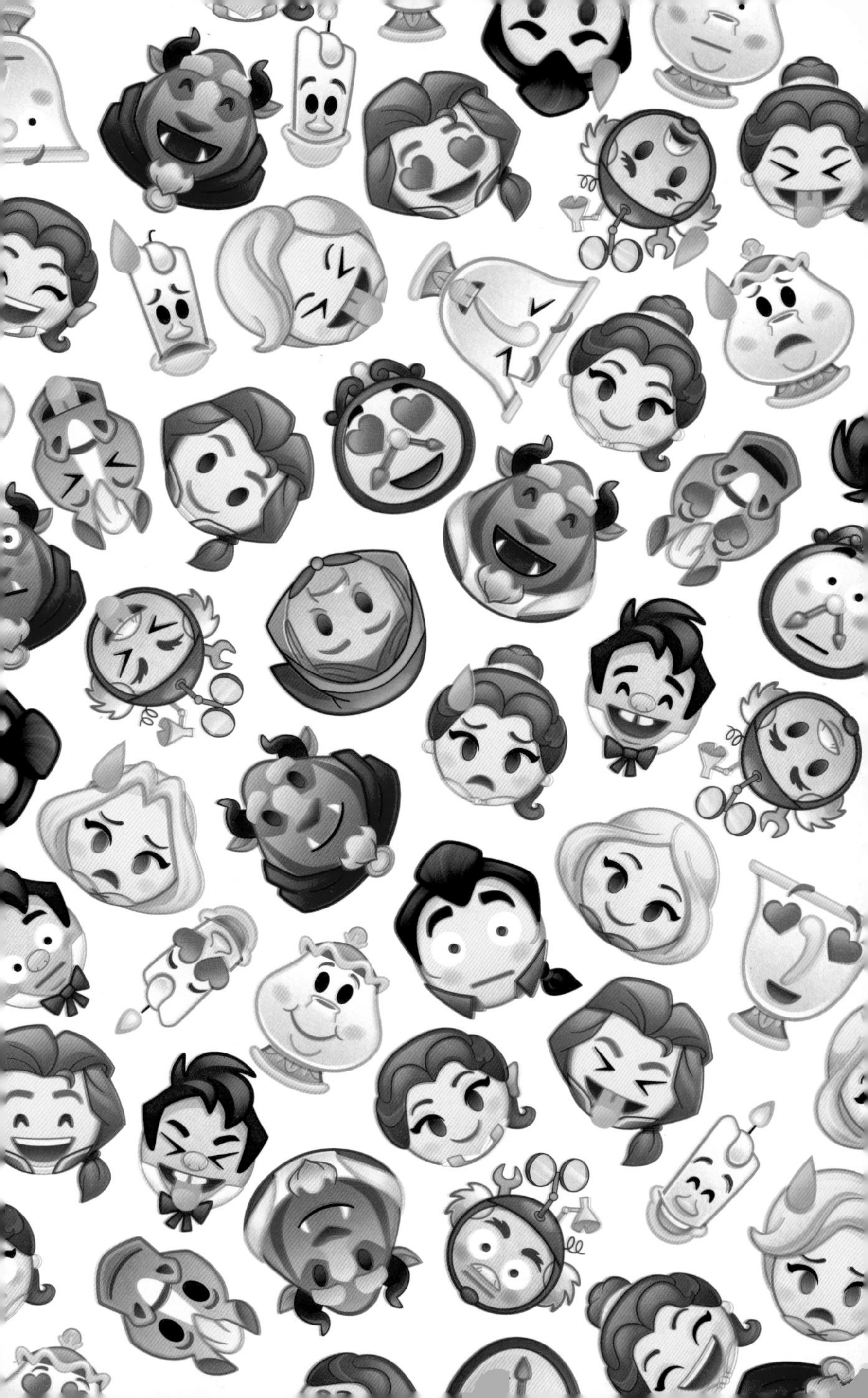

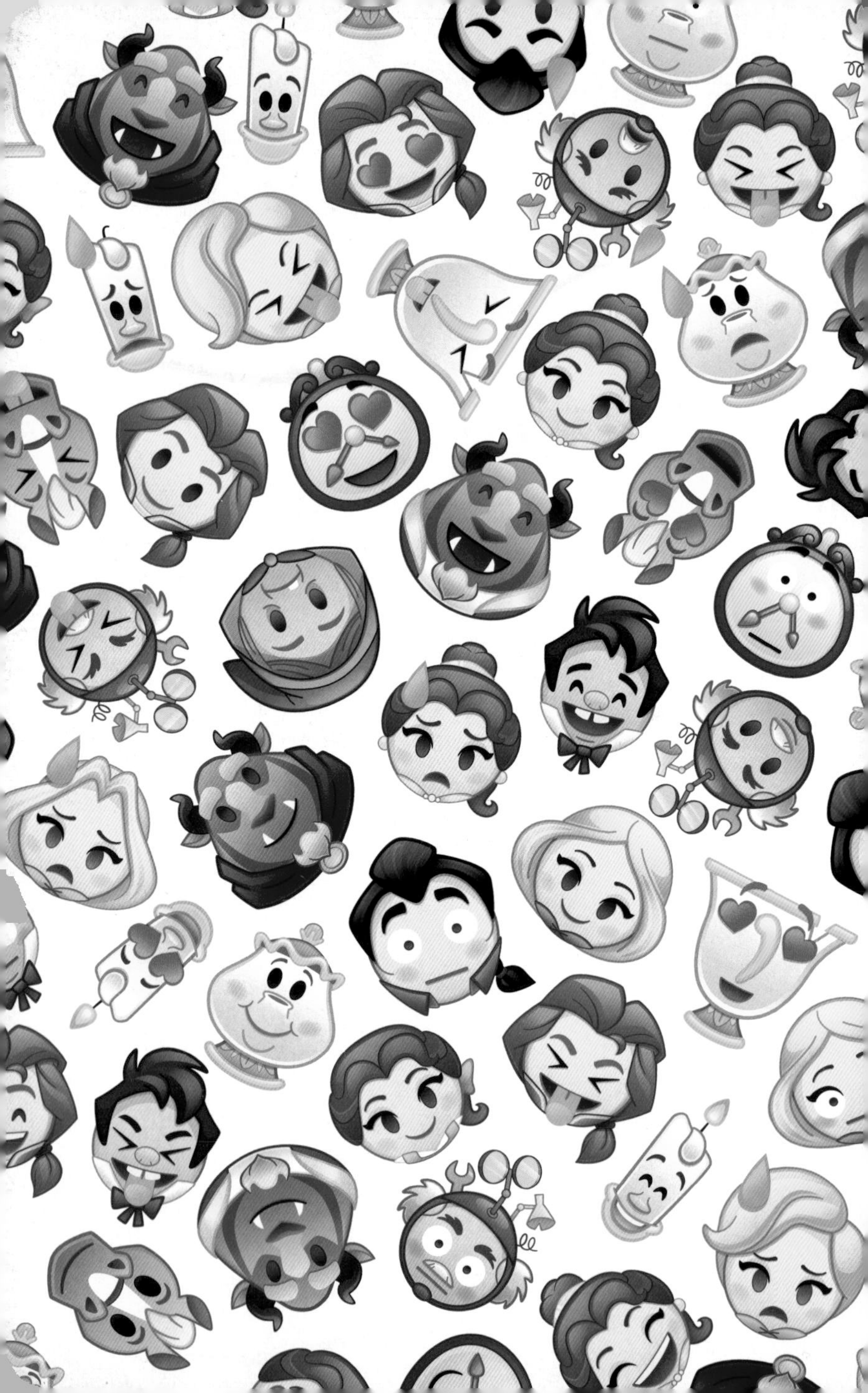

DISNEY

Beauty and the Beast

As Told By

Disney emoji

JOE BOOKS

Published simultaneously in the United States and Canada by Joe Books Ltd
489 College Street, Suite 203, Toronto, ON M6G 1A5

www.joebooks.com

First Joe Books edition: September 2017

Print ISBN: 978-1-77275-552-7

ebook ISBN: 978-1-77275-787-3

Library and Archives Canada Cataloguing in Publication information is available upon request.

Printed and bound in Canada

1 3 5 7 9 10 8 6 4 2

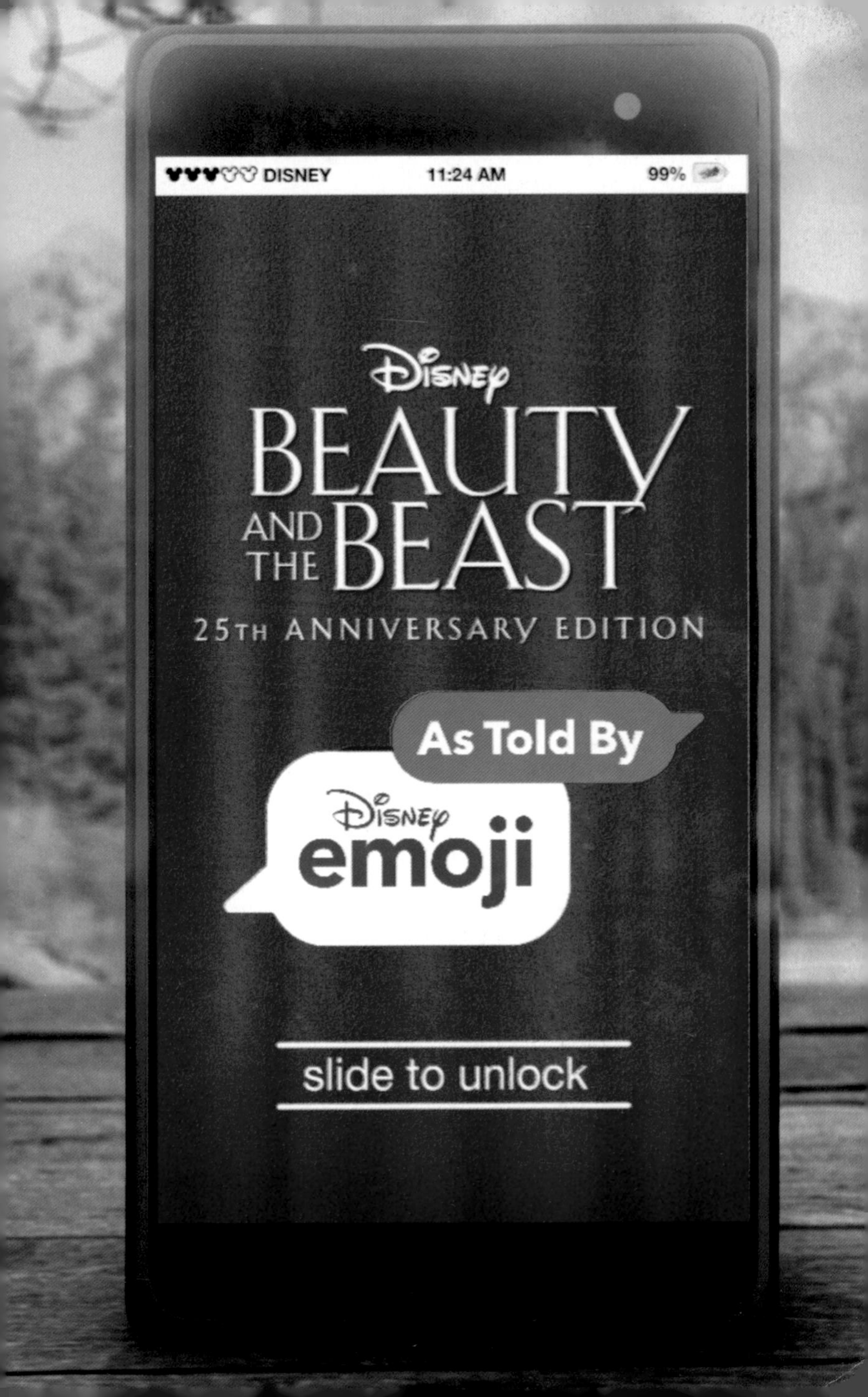
DISNEY
11:24 AM
99%
Disney
BEAUTY AND THE BEAST
25TH ANNIVERSARY EDITION
As Told By
Disney emoji
slide to unlock

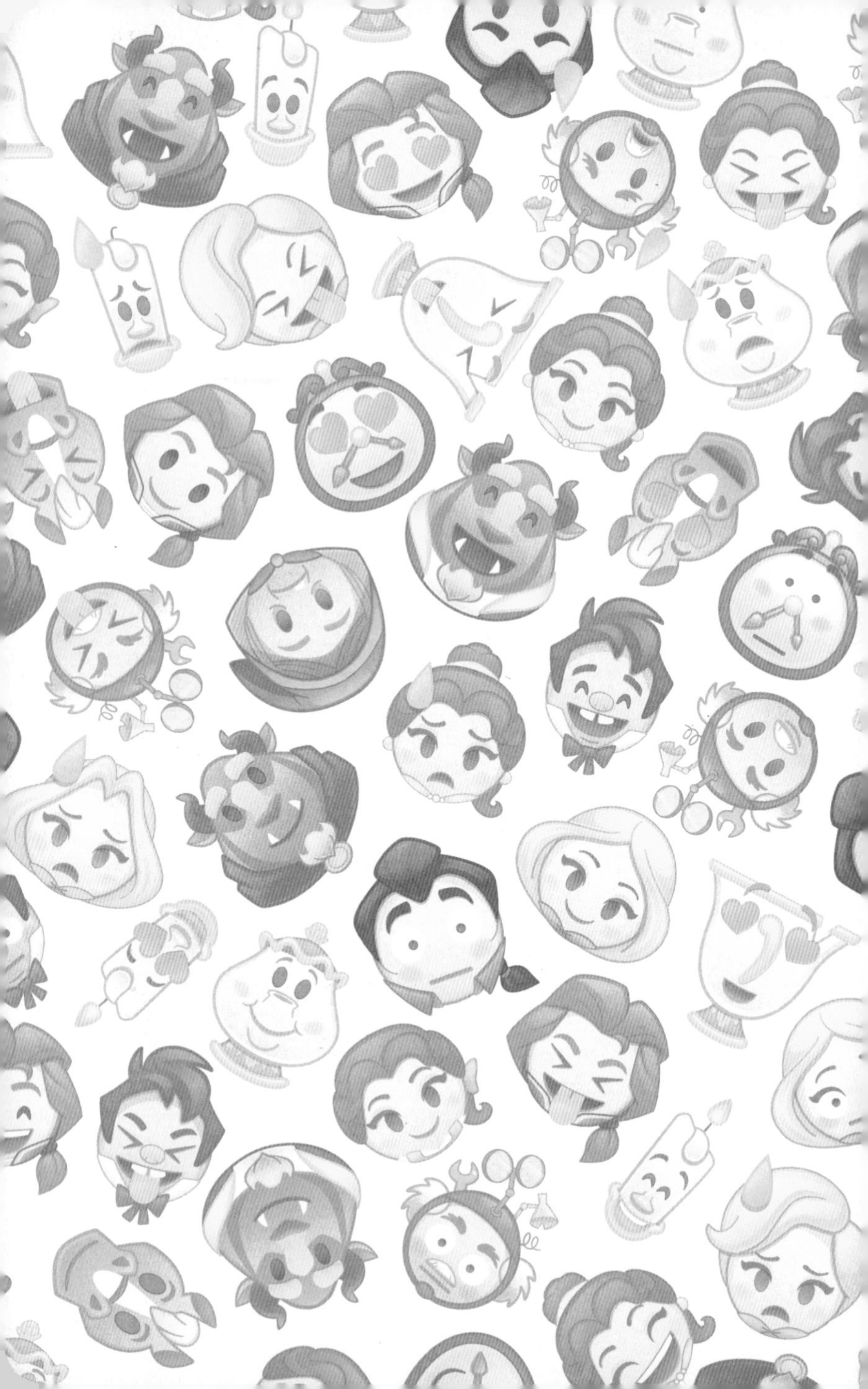

DISNEY 100%

Once upon a time in a faraway land

An arrogant prince lived in a shining castle

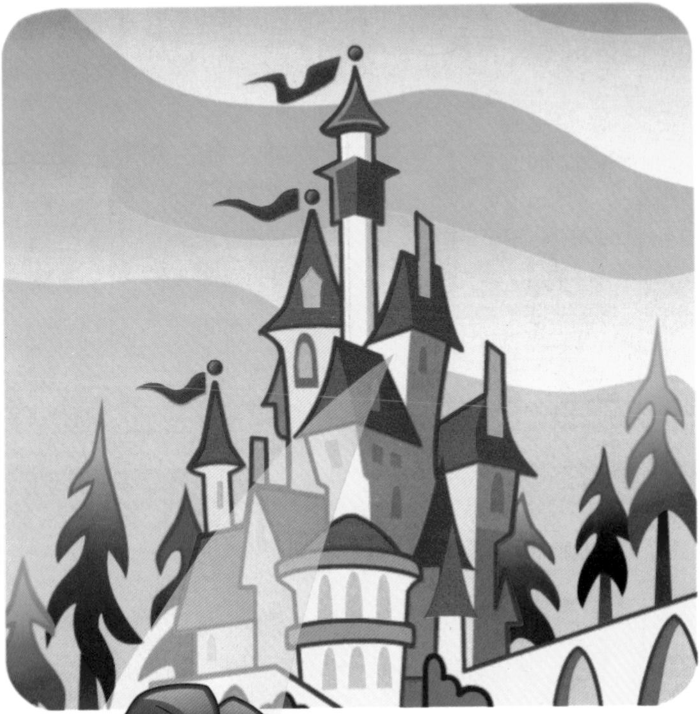

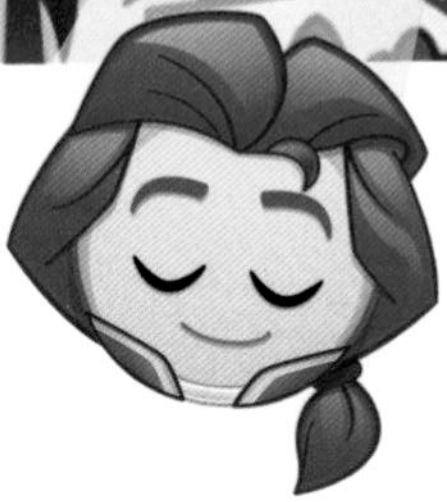

SEND

One winter's night, a beggar woman came to the castle

Her ugliness melted away to reveal a beautiful enchantress

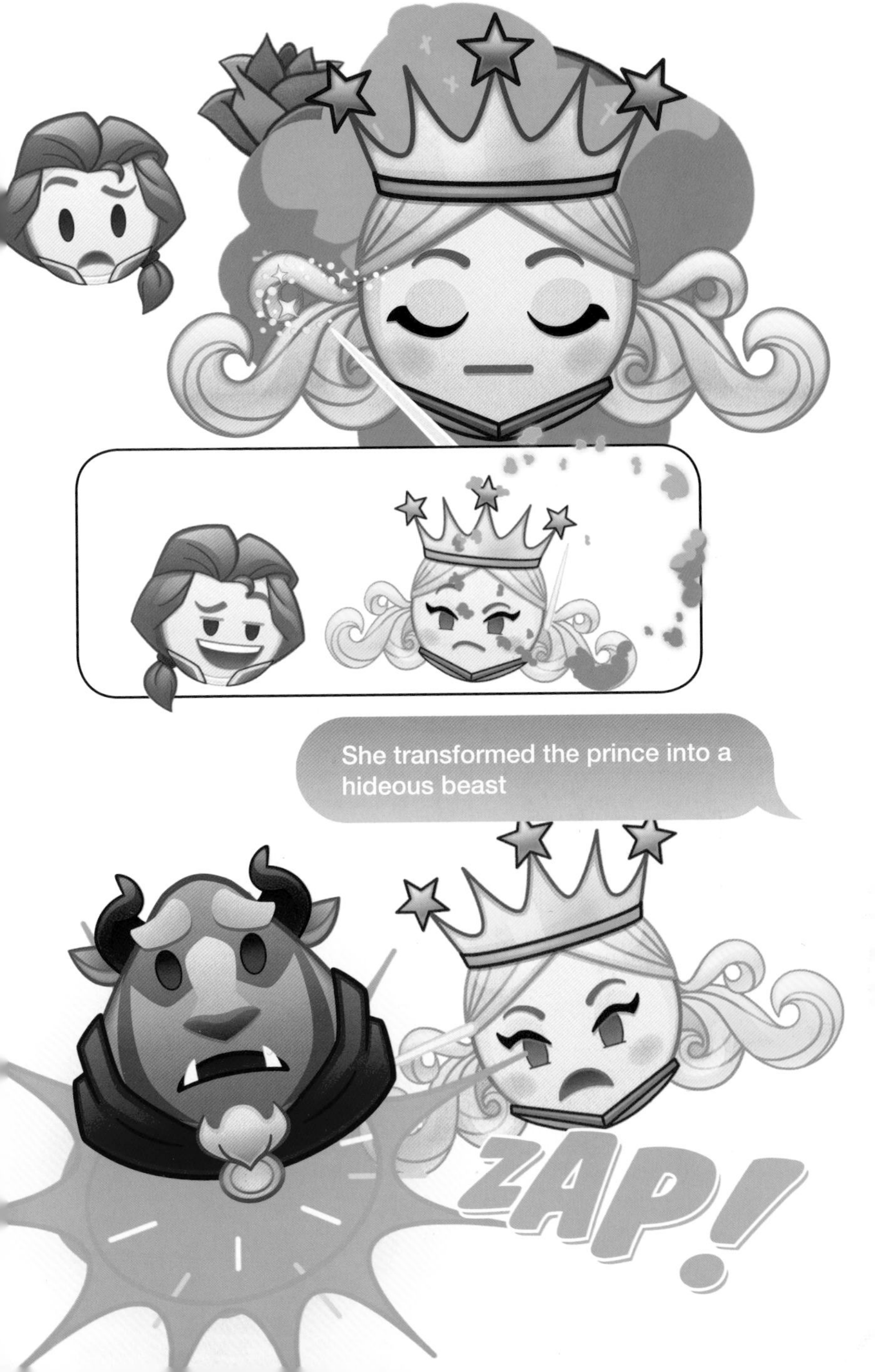
She transformed the prince into a hideous beast
ZAP!

The rose was truly an enchanted rose, which would bloom until his 21st year

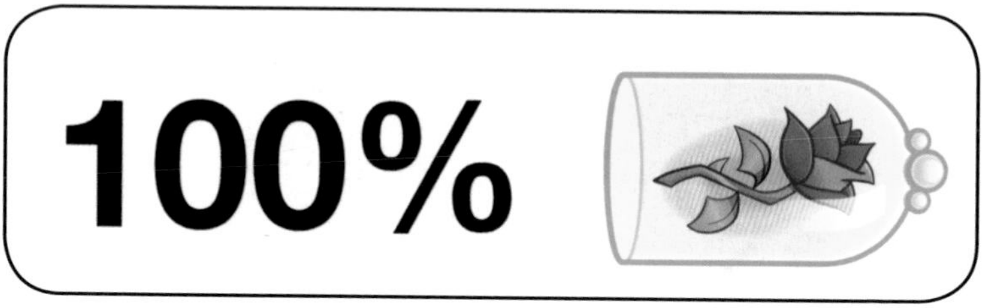

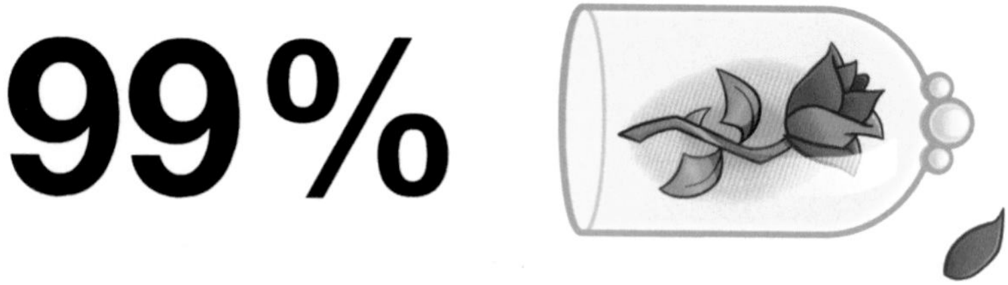

If he could learn to love another by the time the last petal fell, then the spell would be broken

If not, he would be doomed to remain a beast forever

99% 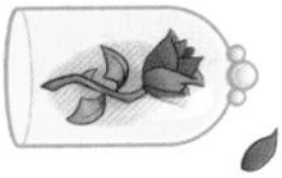

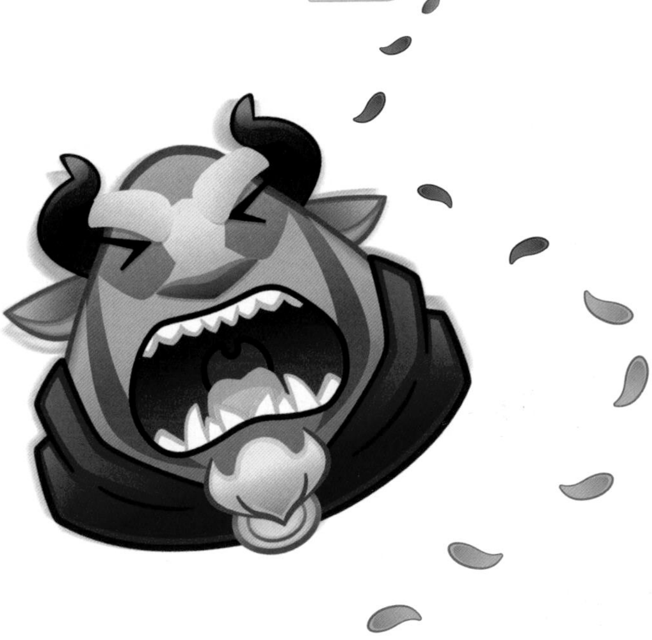

RAWR

0:06

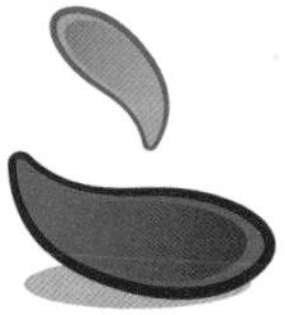

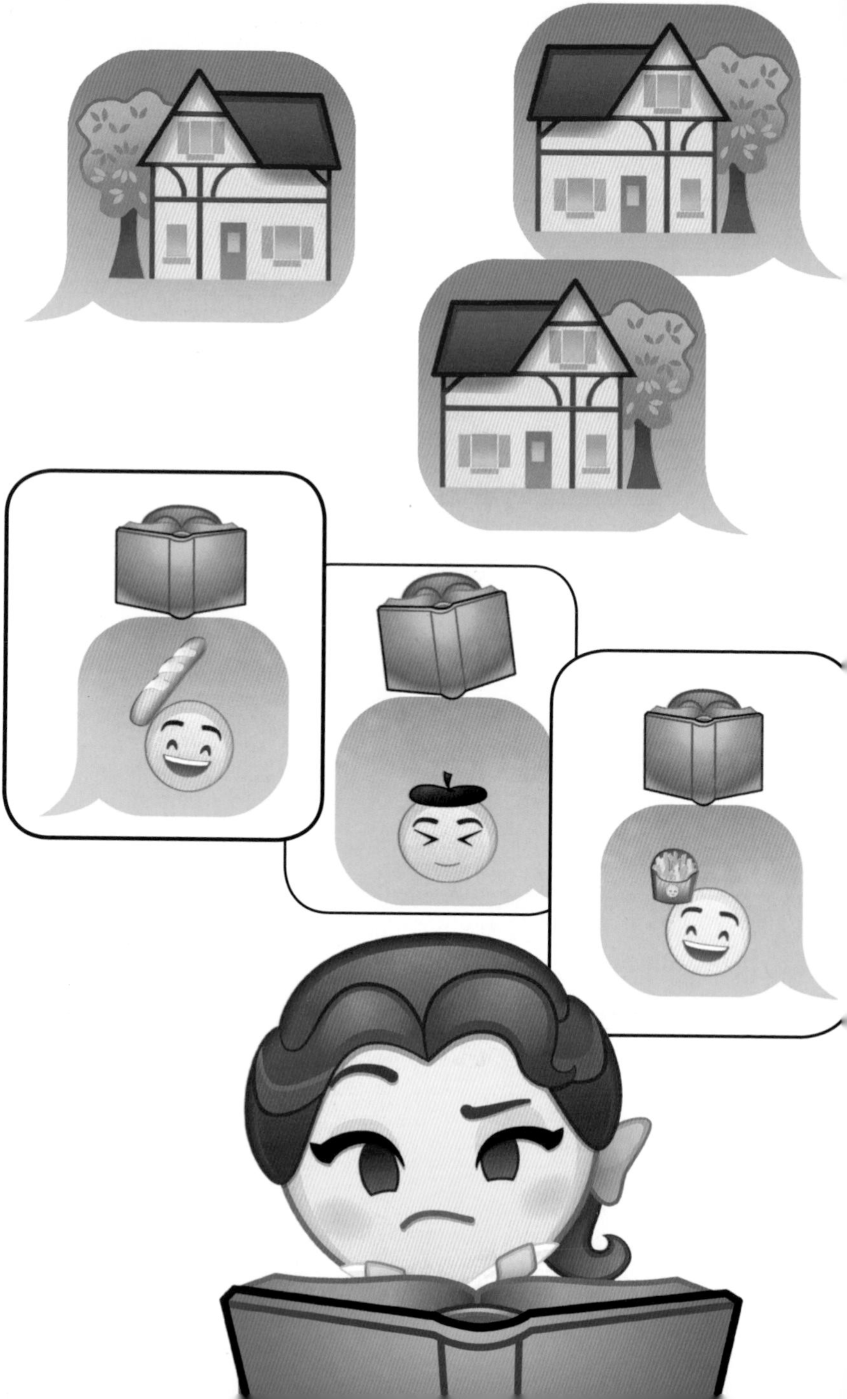

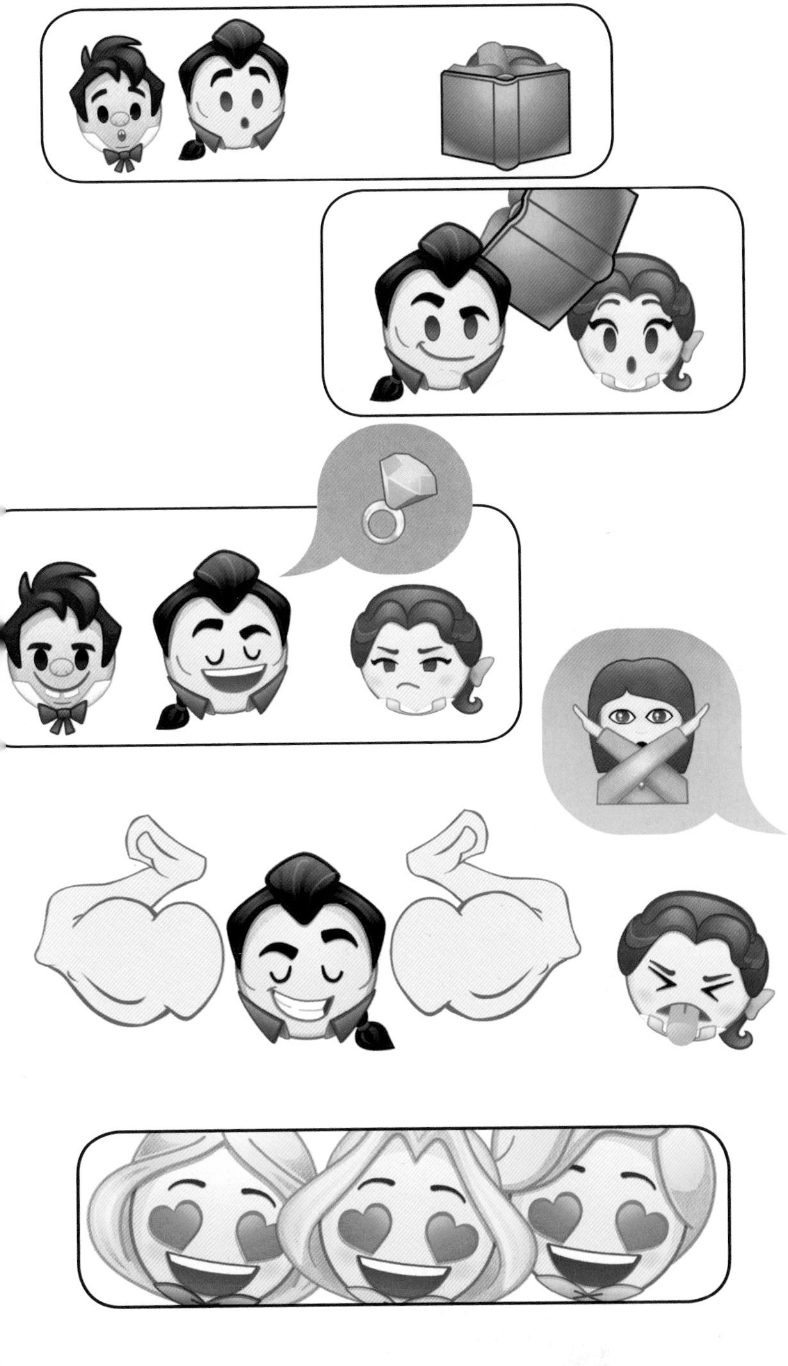

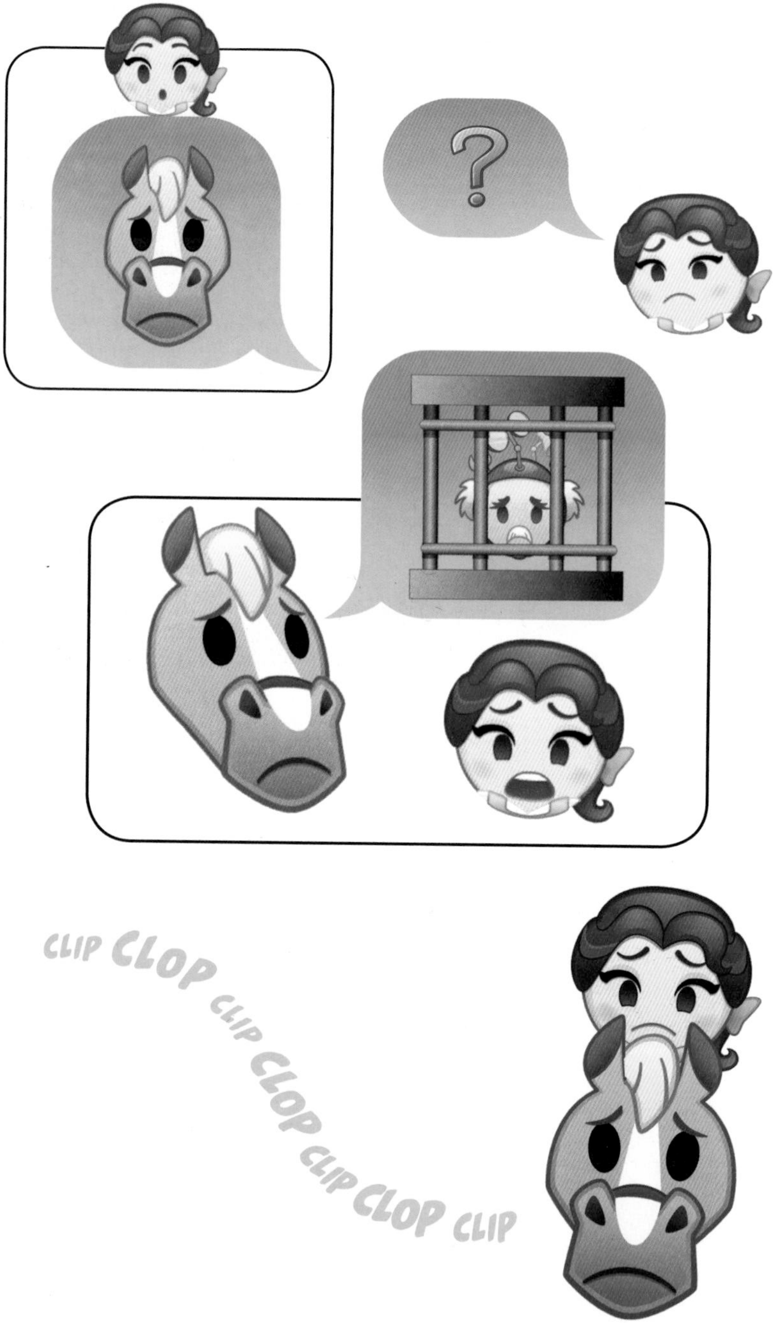
?
CLIP CLOP CLIP CLOP CLIP CLOP CLIP

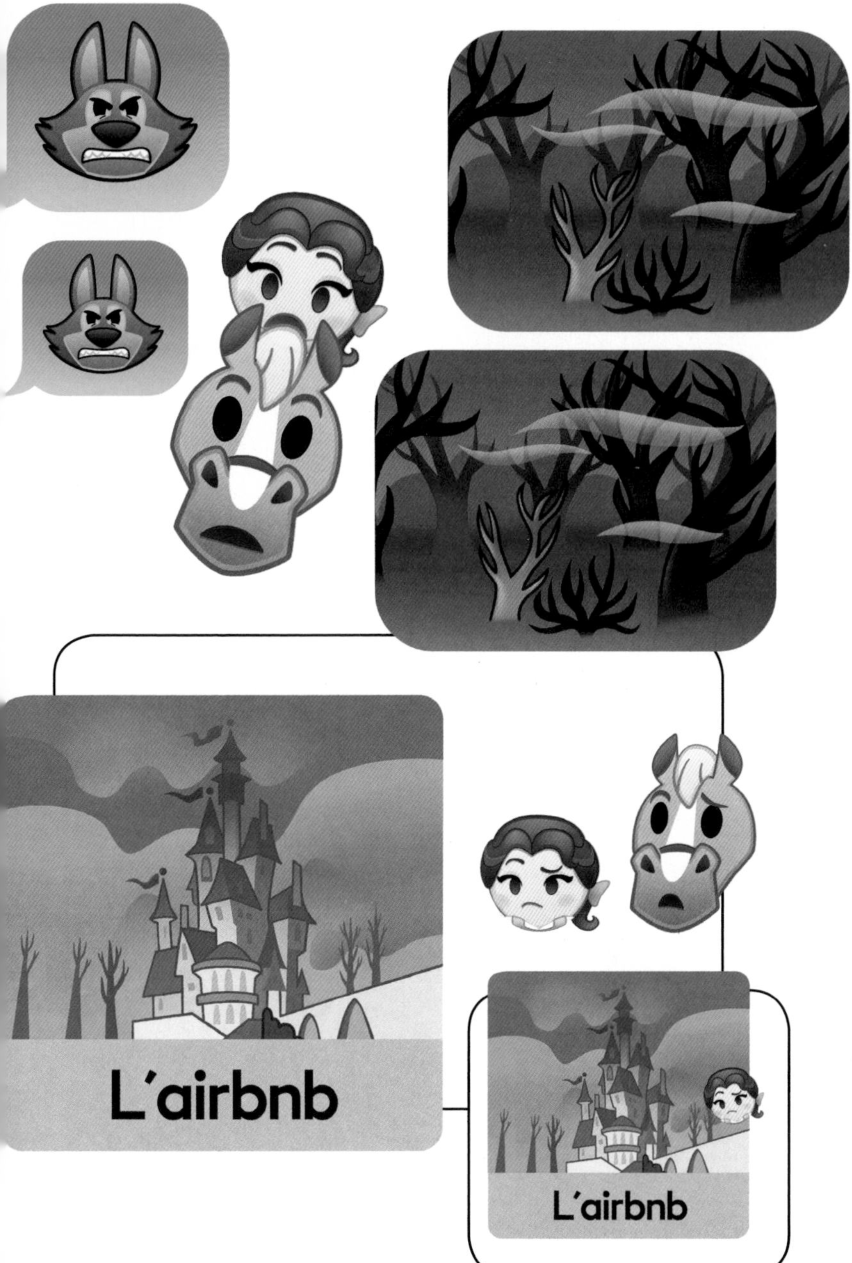
L′airbnb
L′airbnb

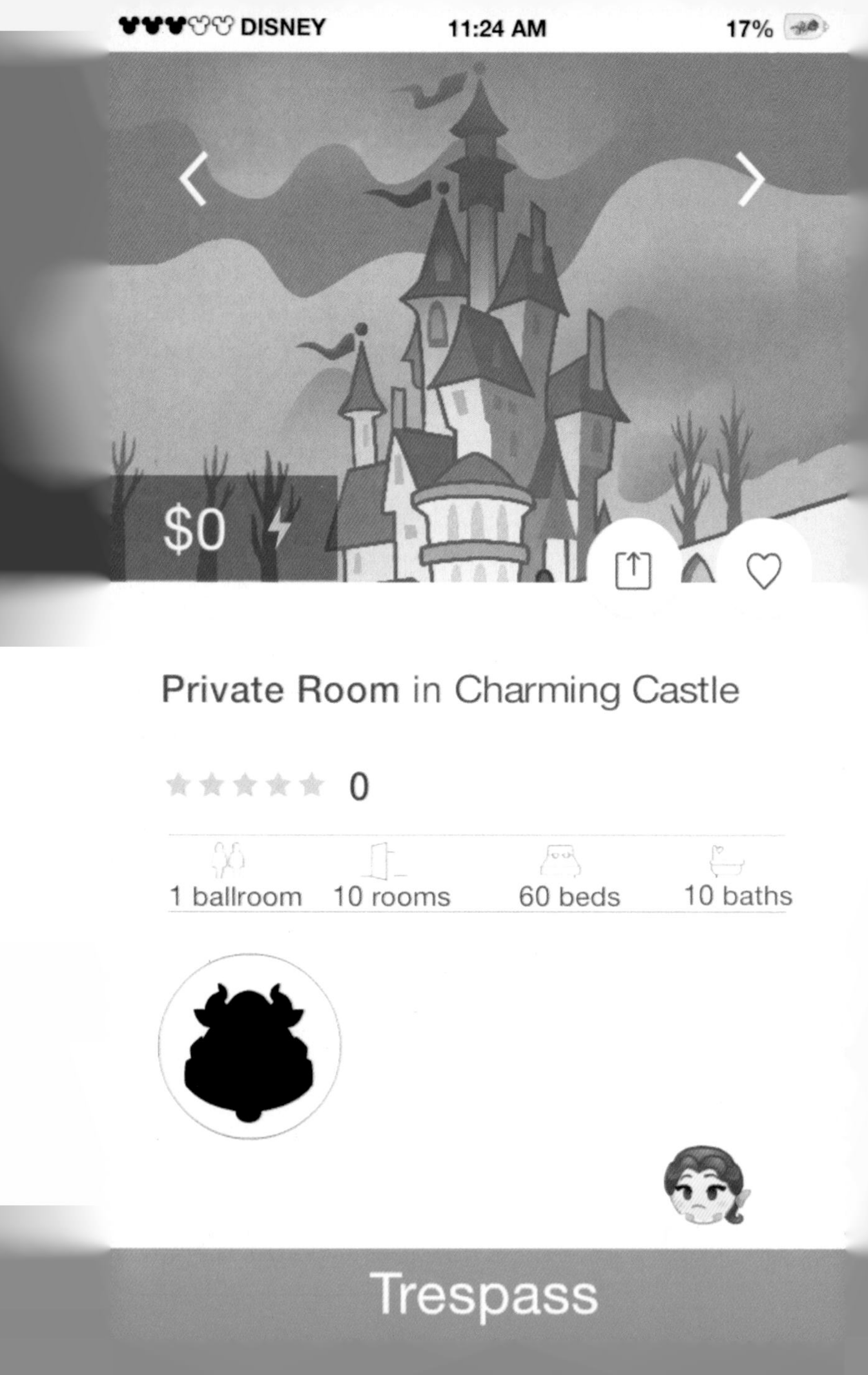
DISNEY
11:24 AM
17%
$0
Private Room in Charming Castle
0
1 ballroom
10 rooms
60 beds
10 baths
Trespass

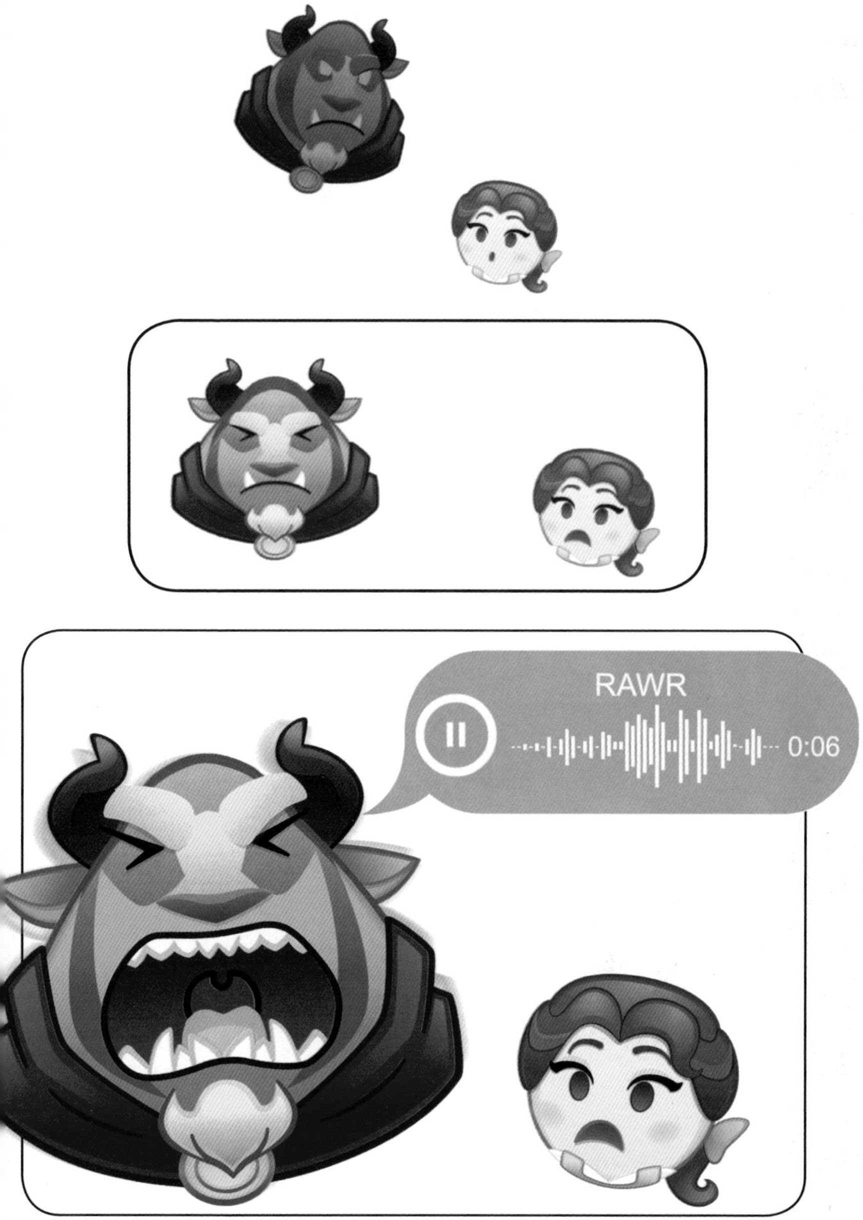
RAWR
0:06

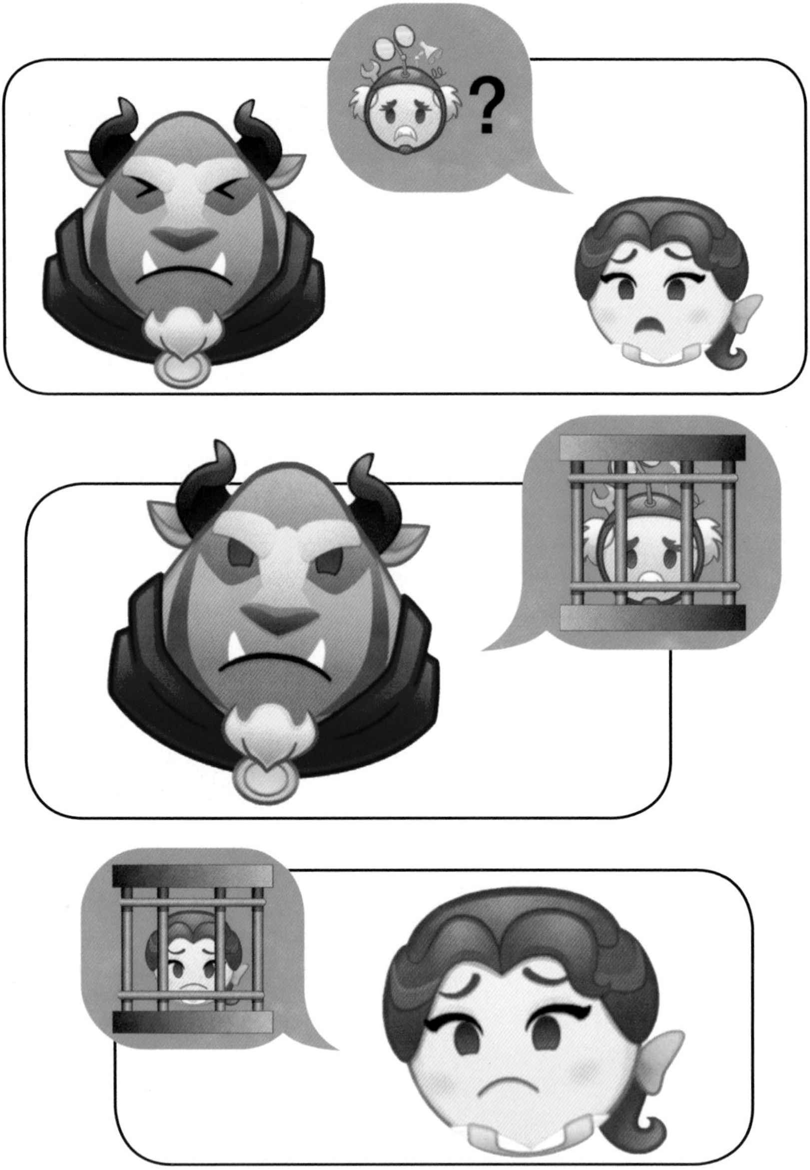
?

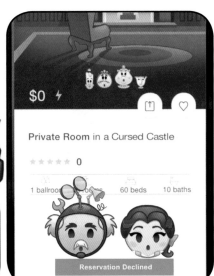

Private Room in a Cursed Castle

★ ★ ★ ★ ★ 0

1 ballroom | ... rooms | 60 beds | 10 baths

Reservation Declined

RAWR
0:06

Belle replaced her father as the Beast's prisoner

GULP

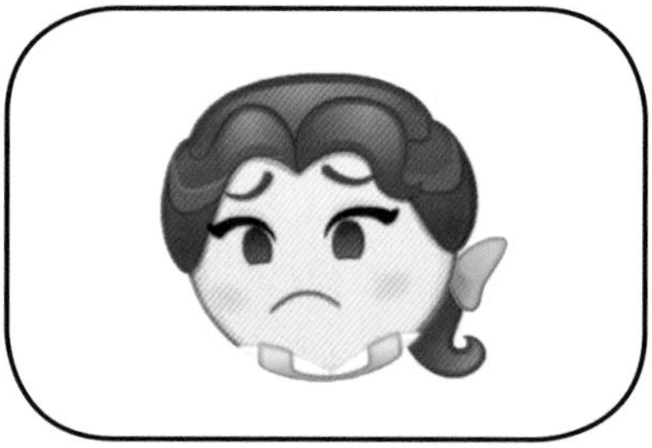

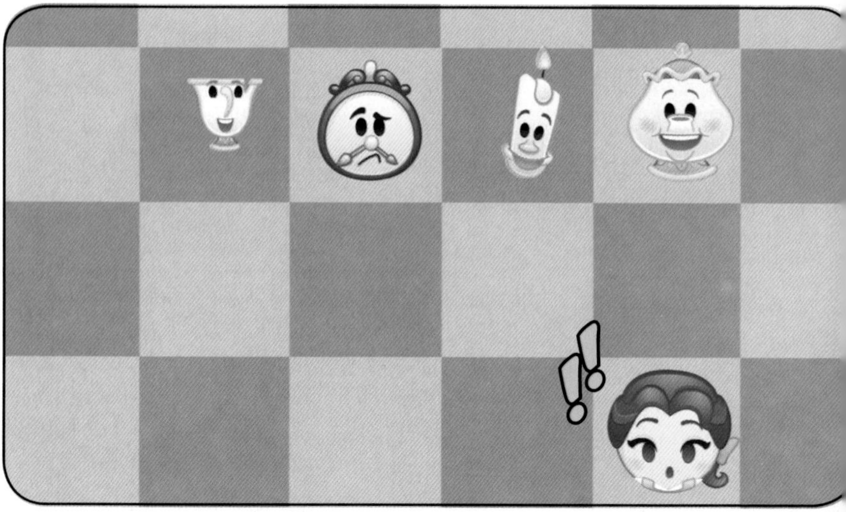

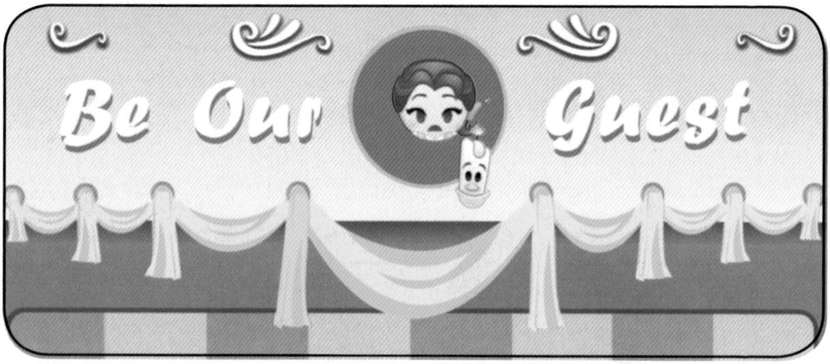
Be Our Guest

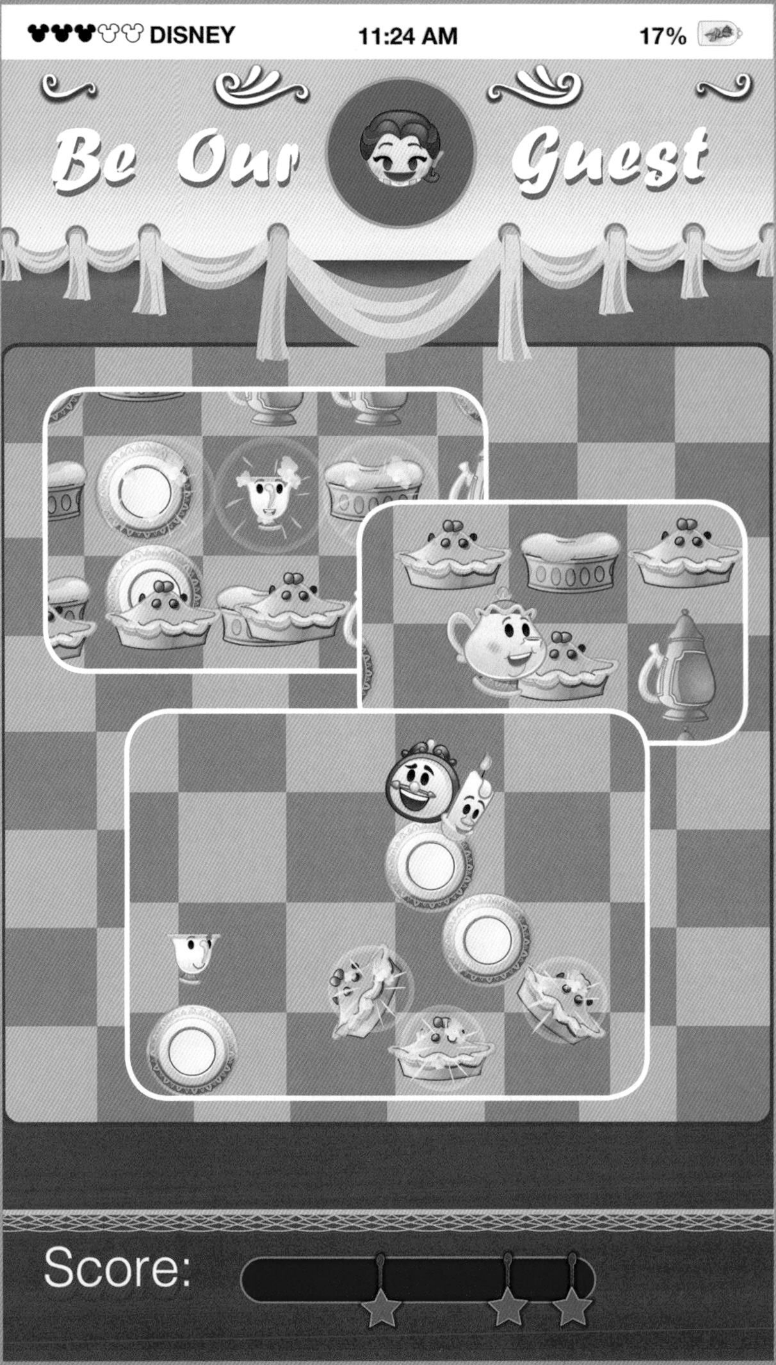
DISNEY
11:24 AM
17%
Be Our Guest
Score:

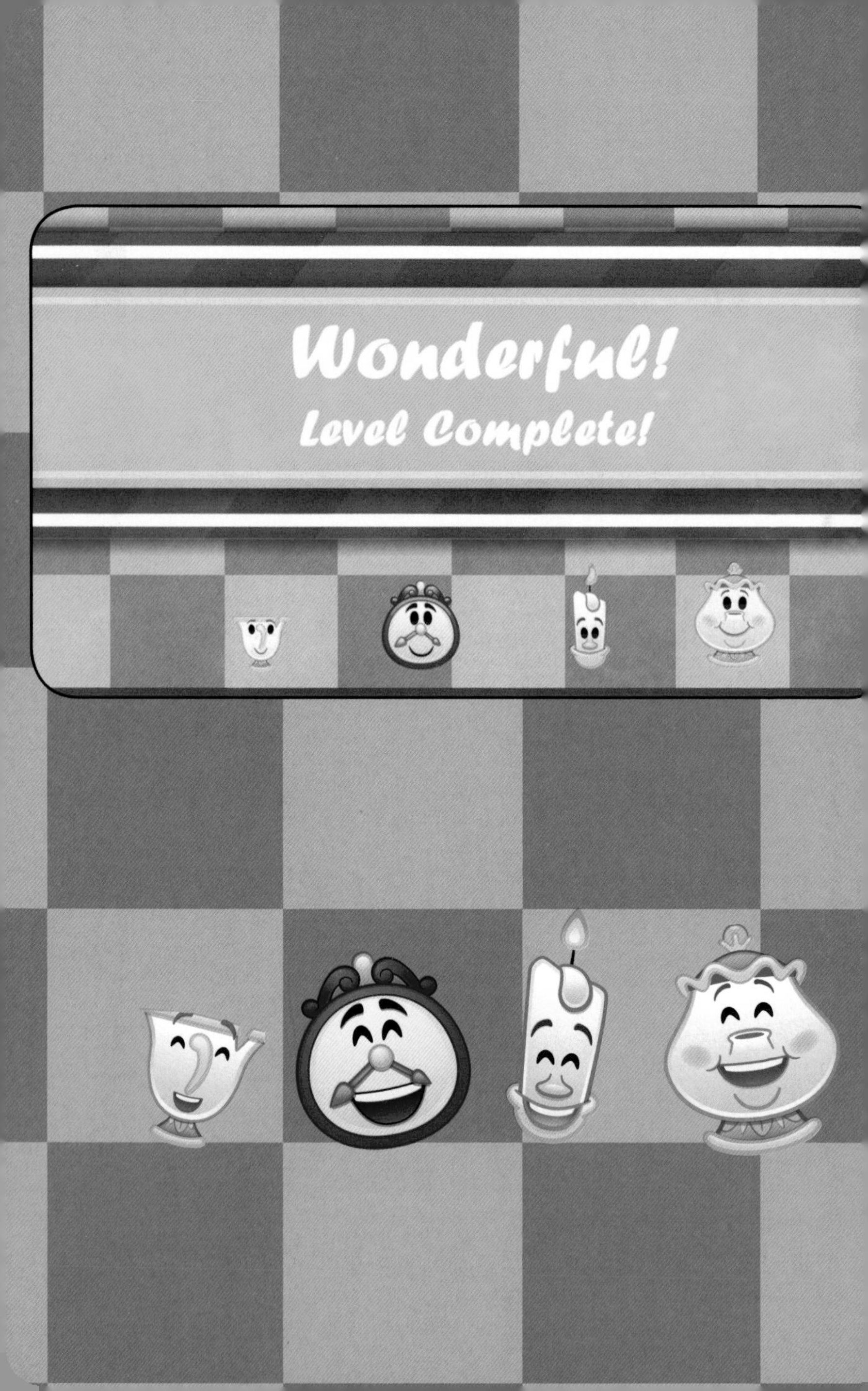
Wonderful!
Level Complete!

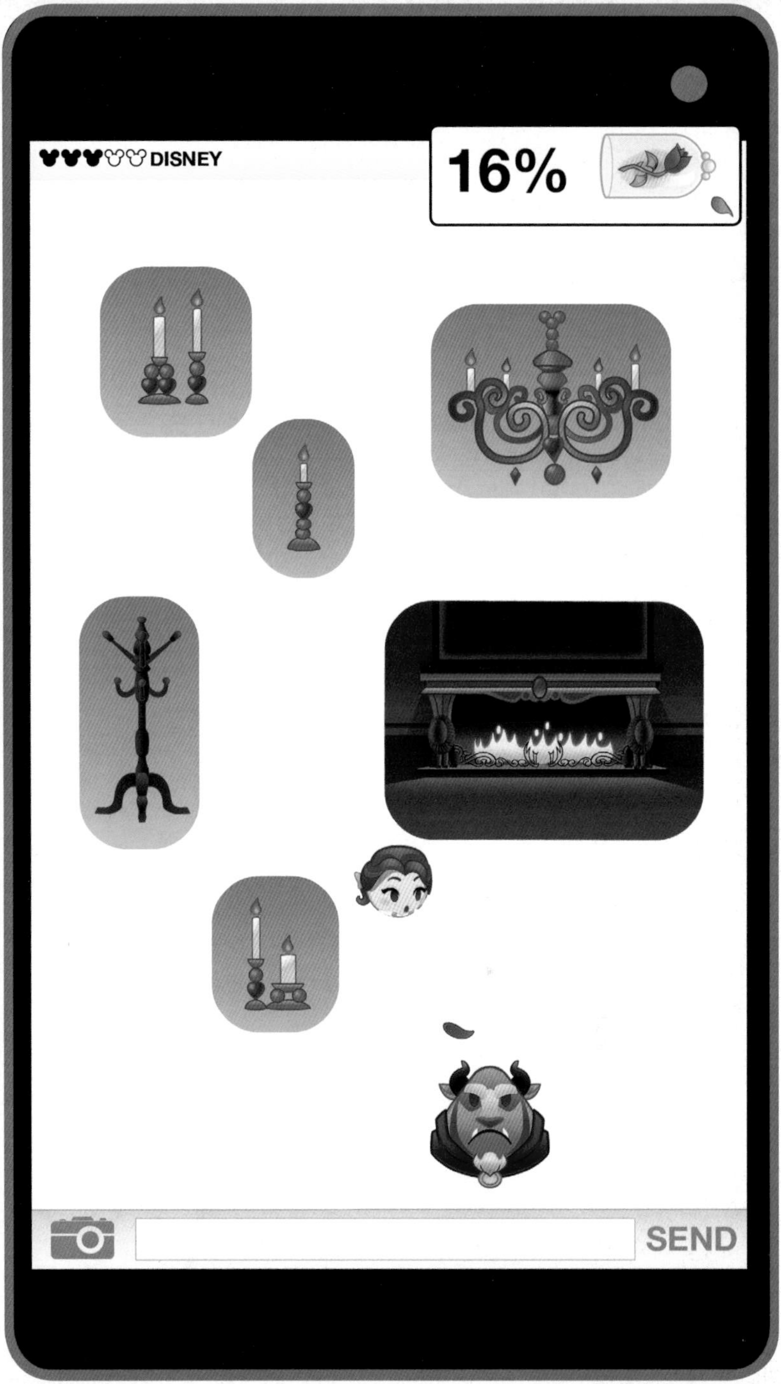

DISNEY
16%
SEND

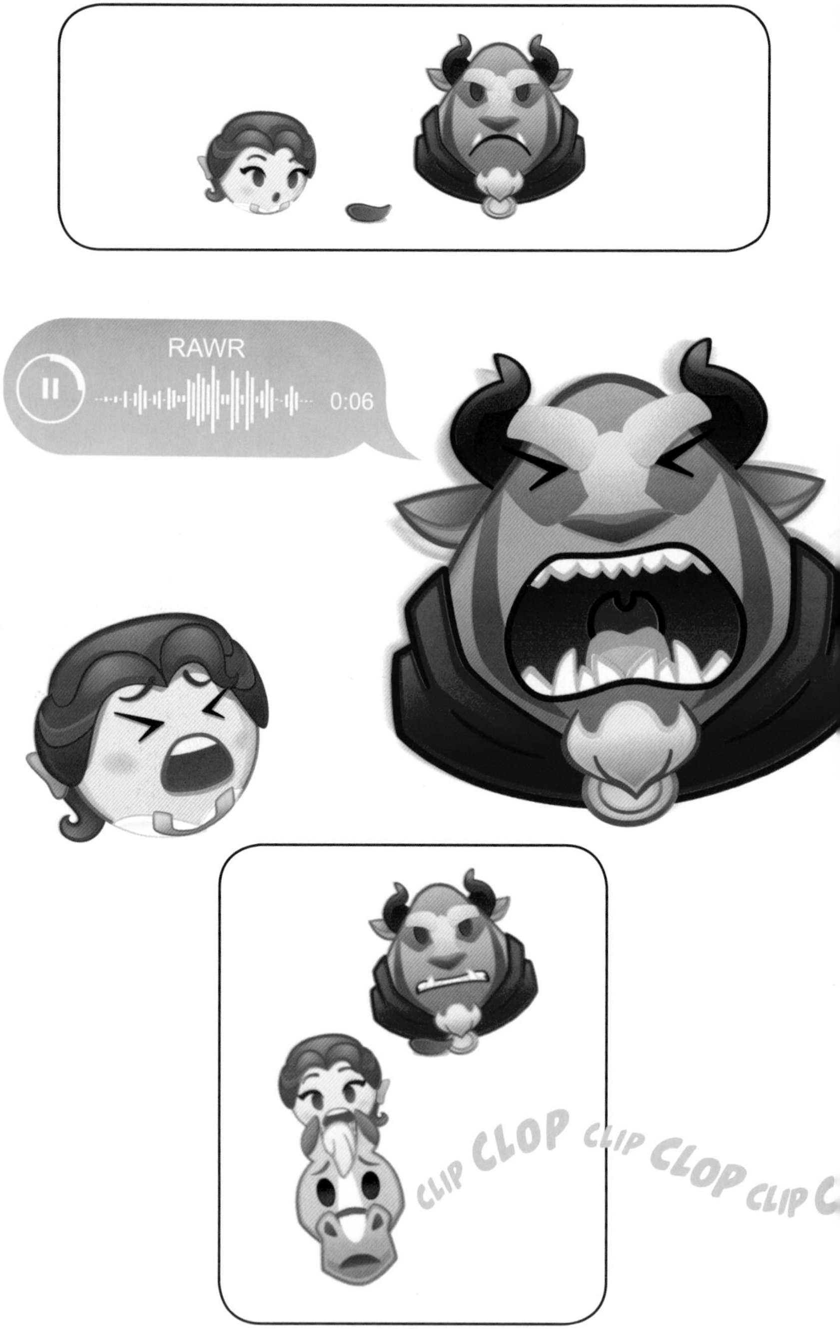
RAWR
0:06
CLIP CLOP CLIP CLOP CLIP

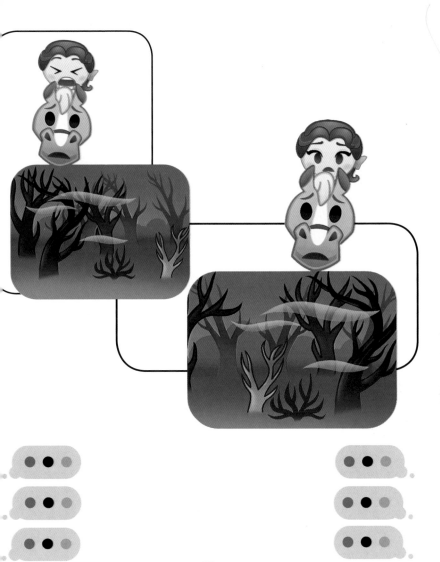

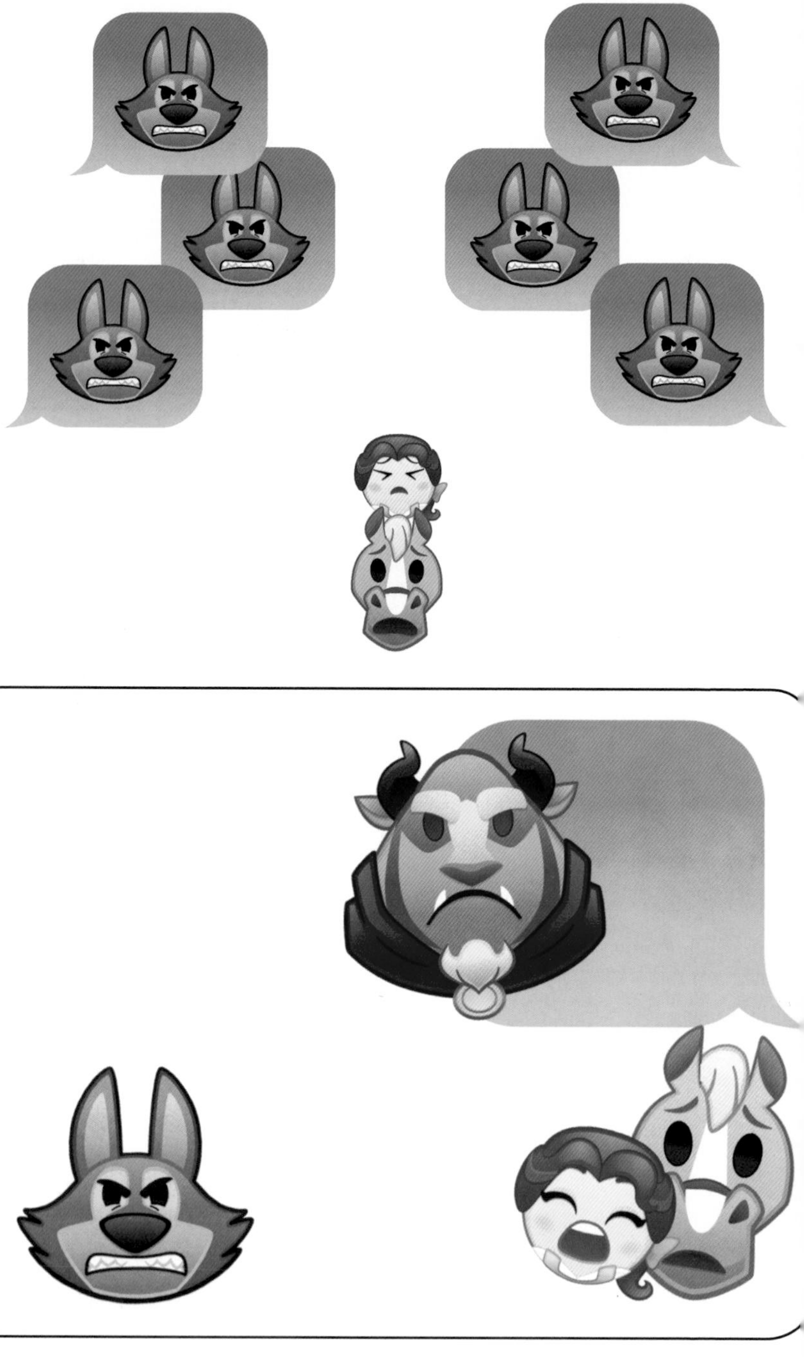

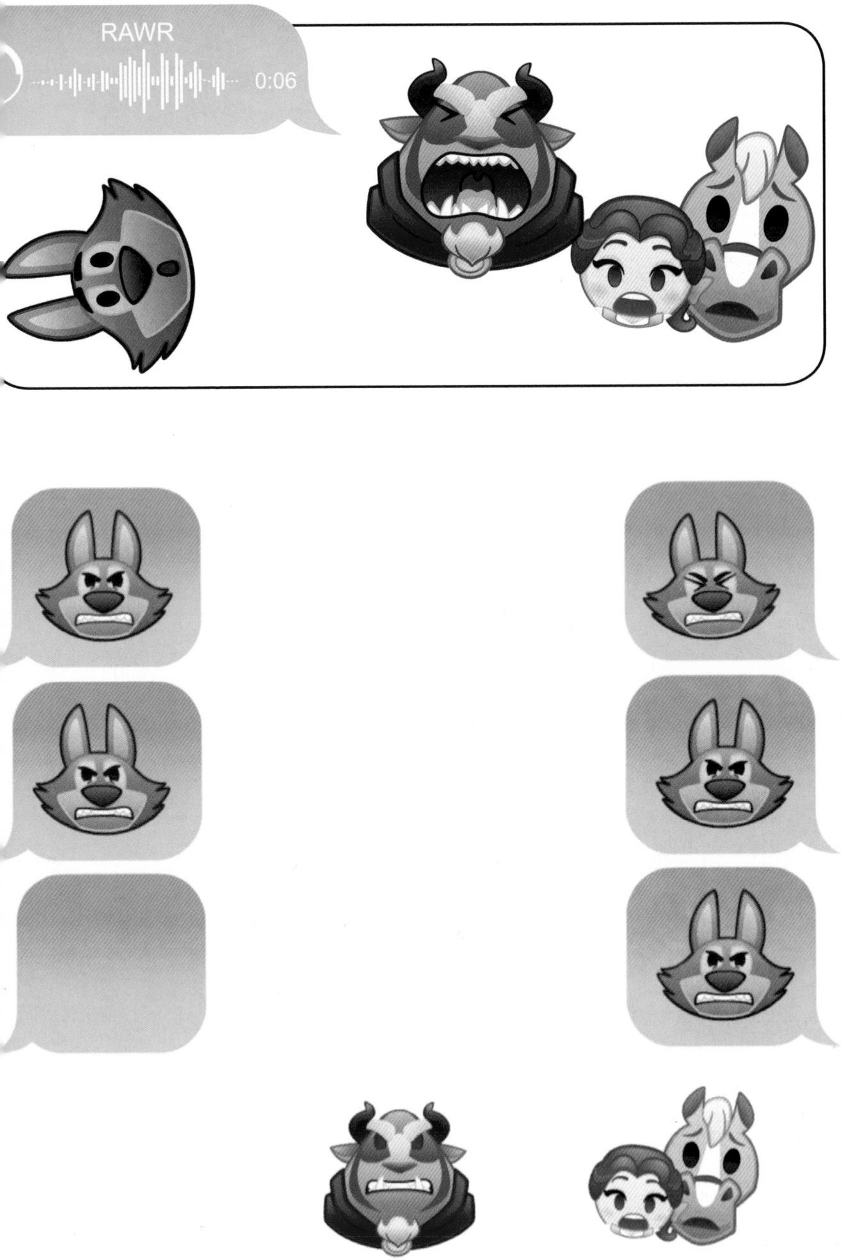
RAWR
0:06

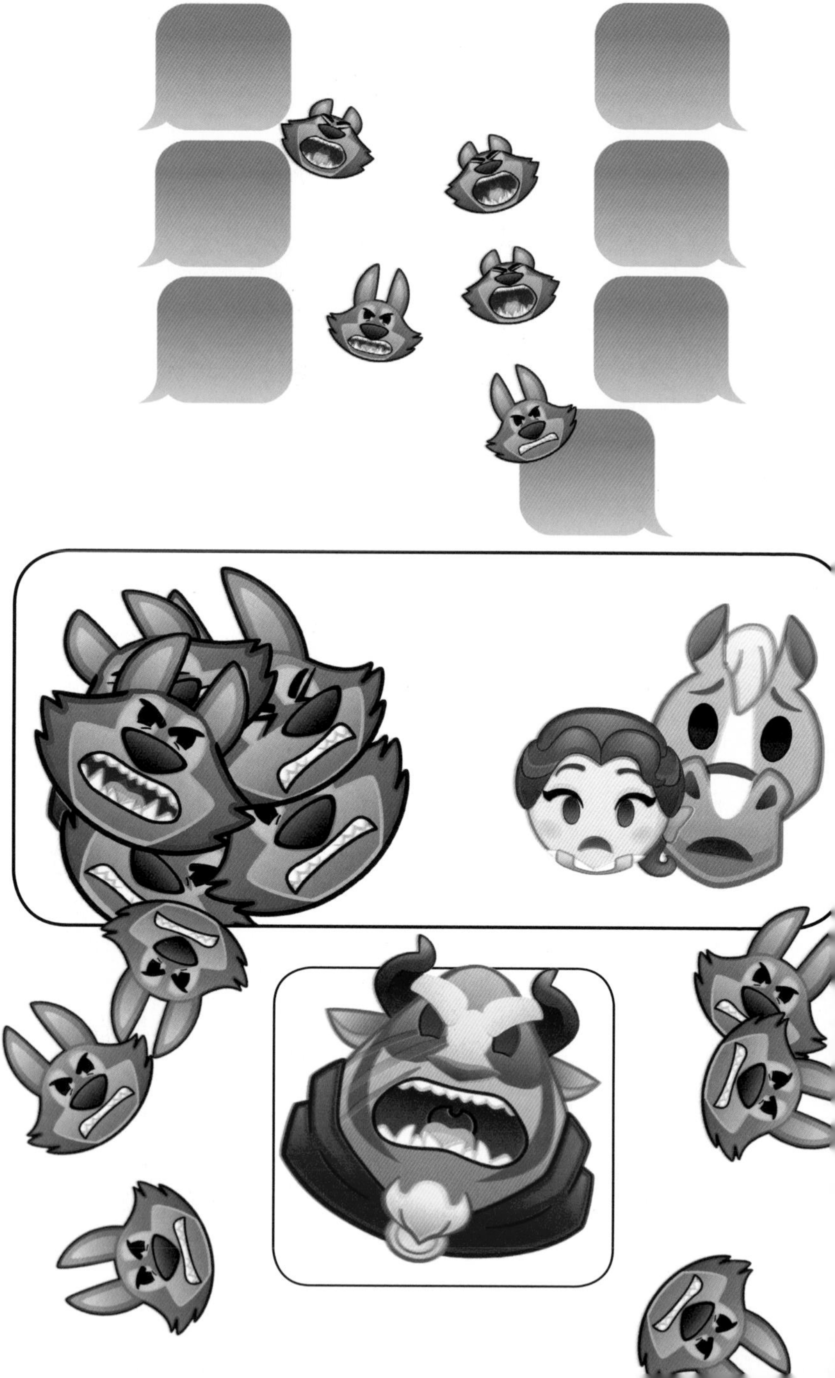

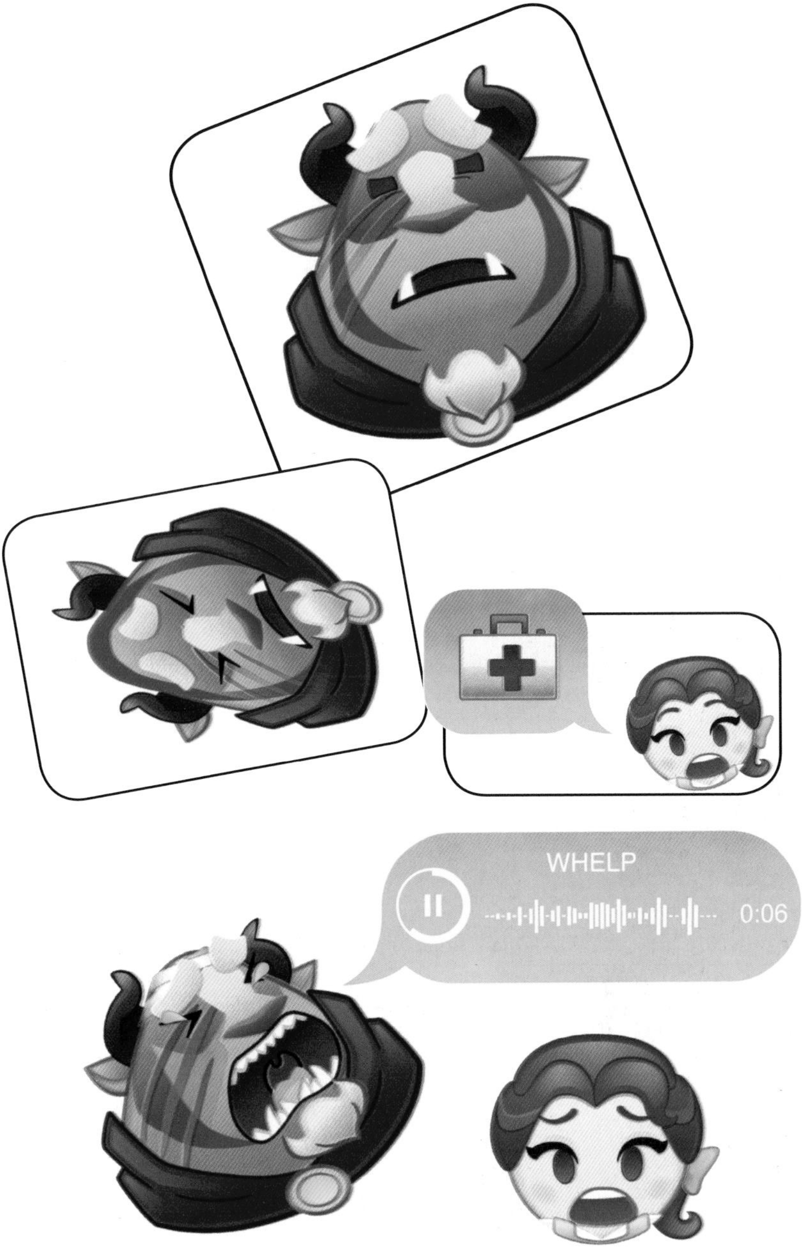
WHELP
0:06

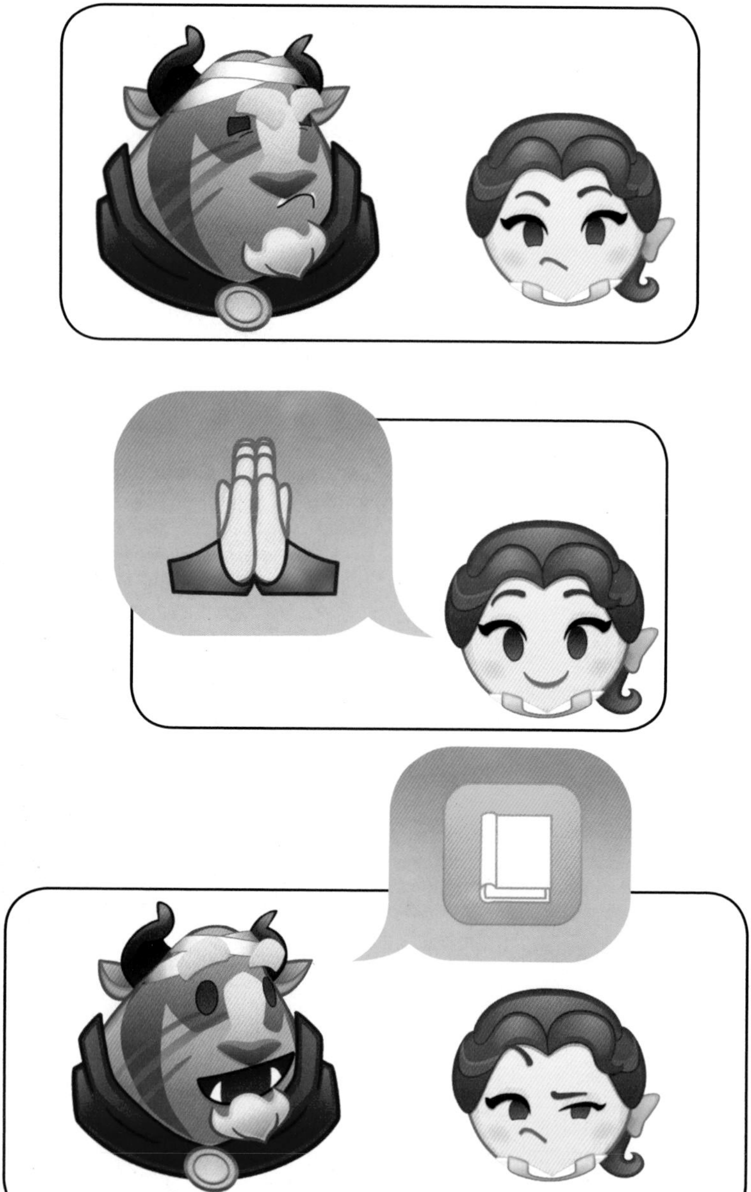

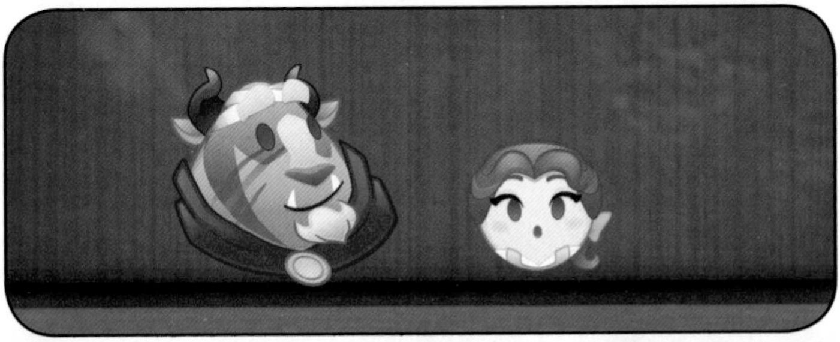

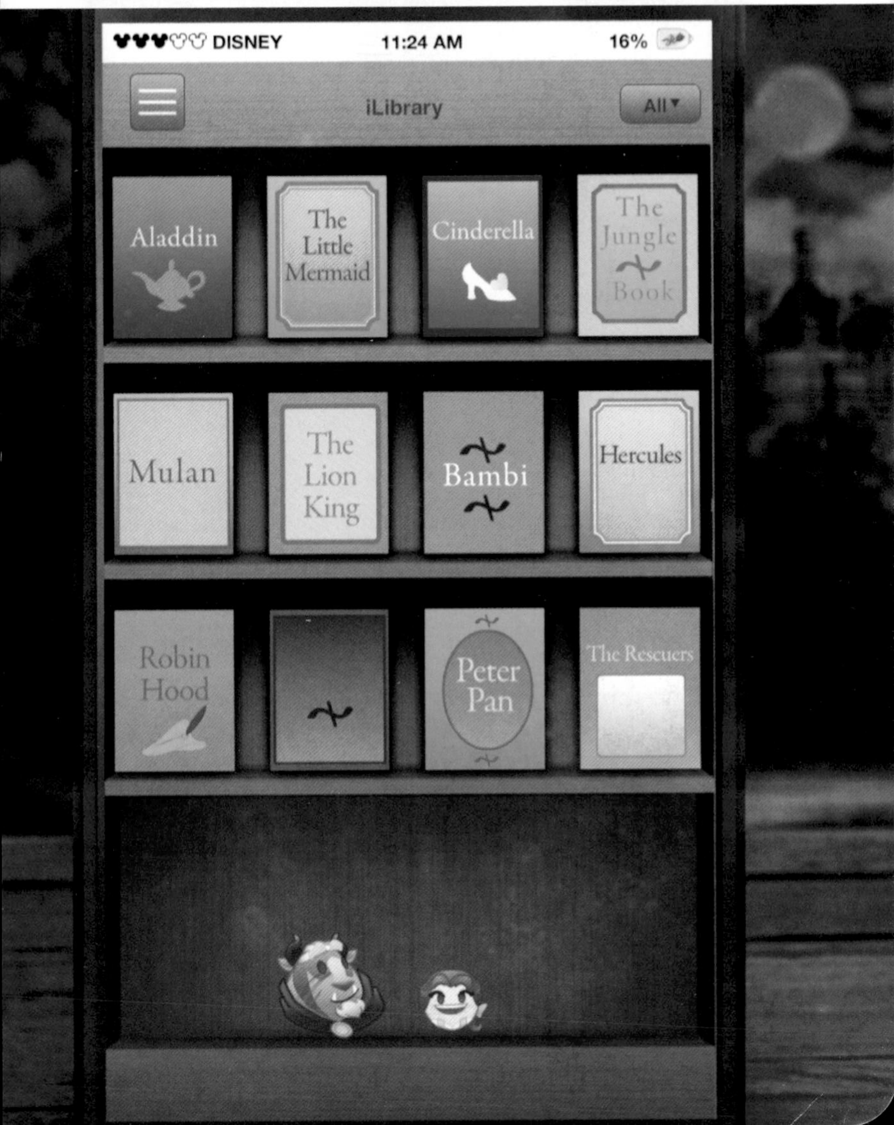

DISNEY
11:24 AM
16%
iLibrary
All
Aladdin
The Little Mermaid
Cinderella
The Jungle Book
Mulan
The Lion King
Bambi
Hercules
Robin Hood
Peter Pan
The Rescuers

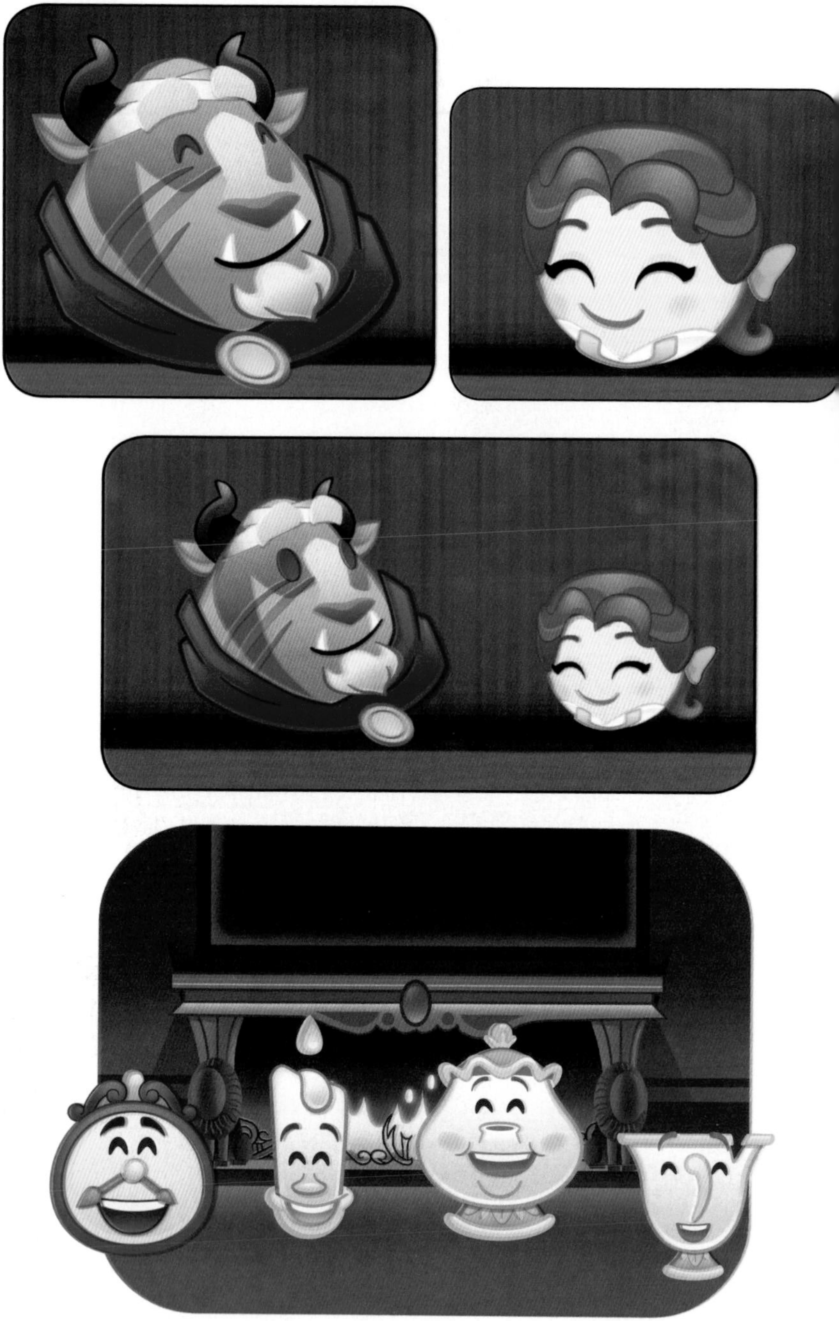

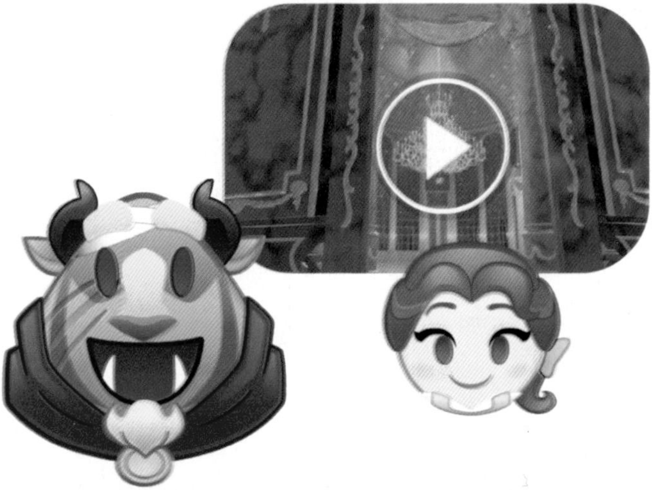

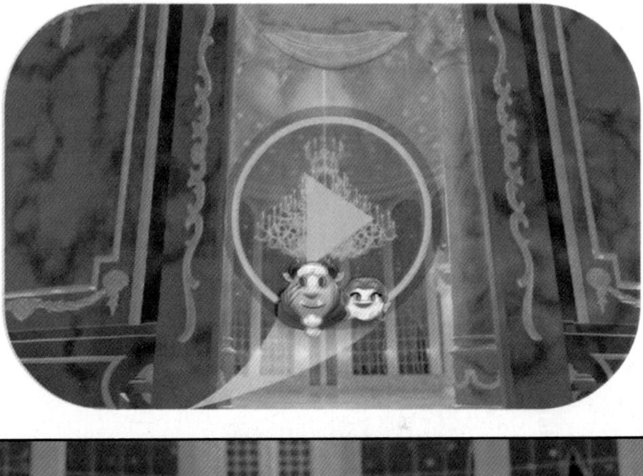

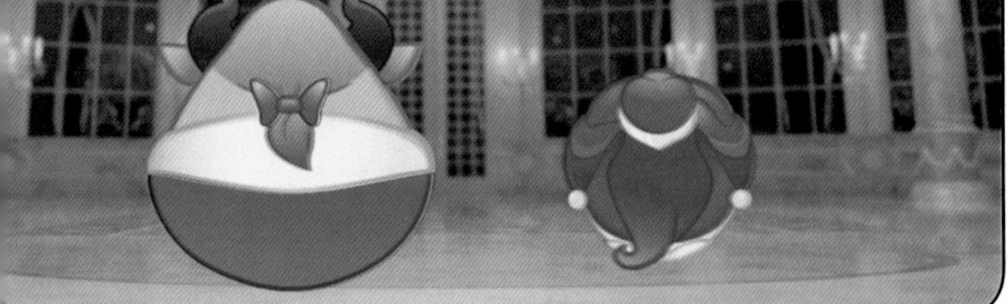

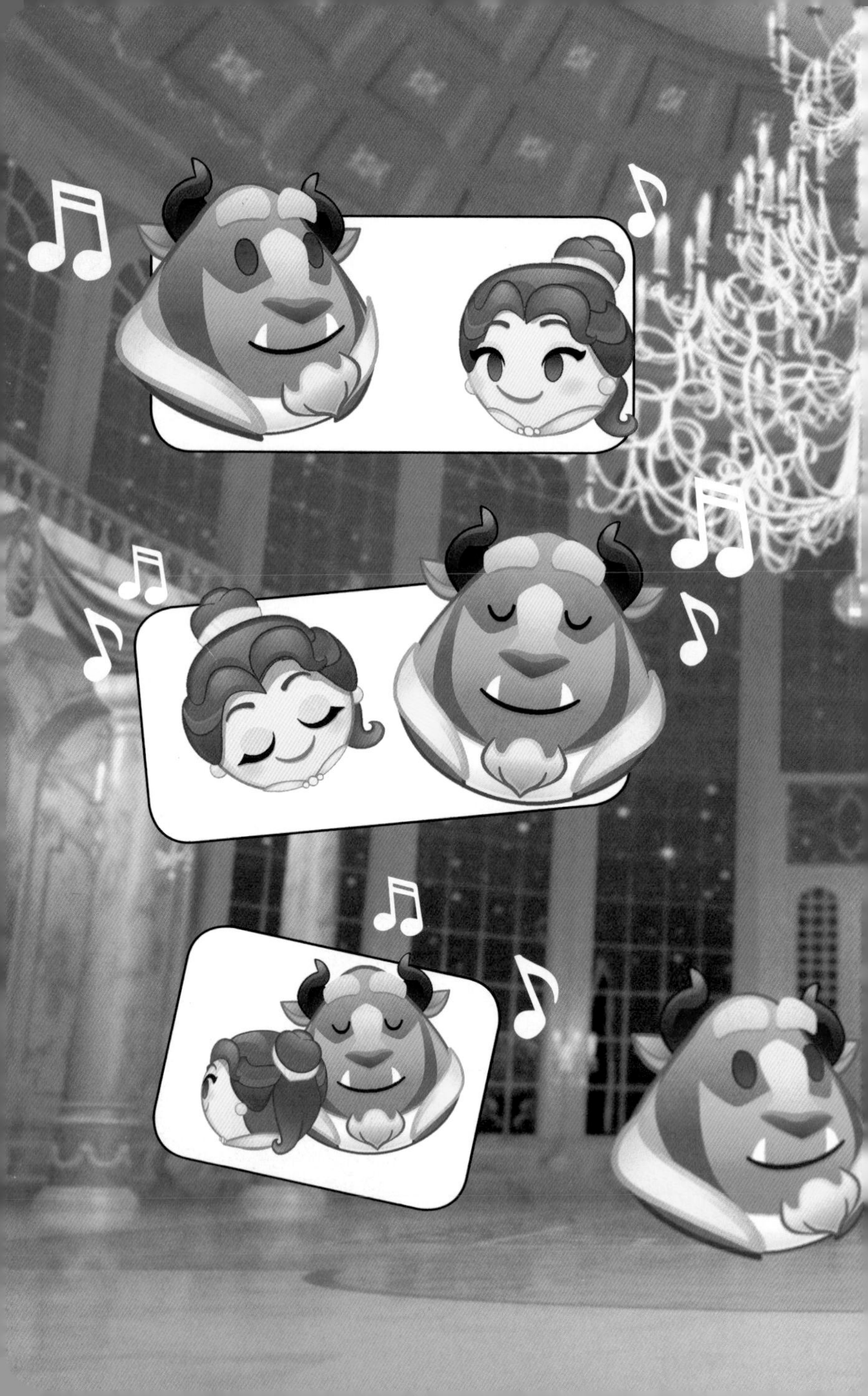

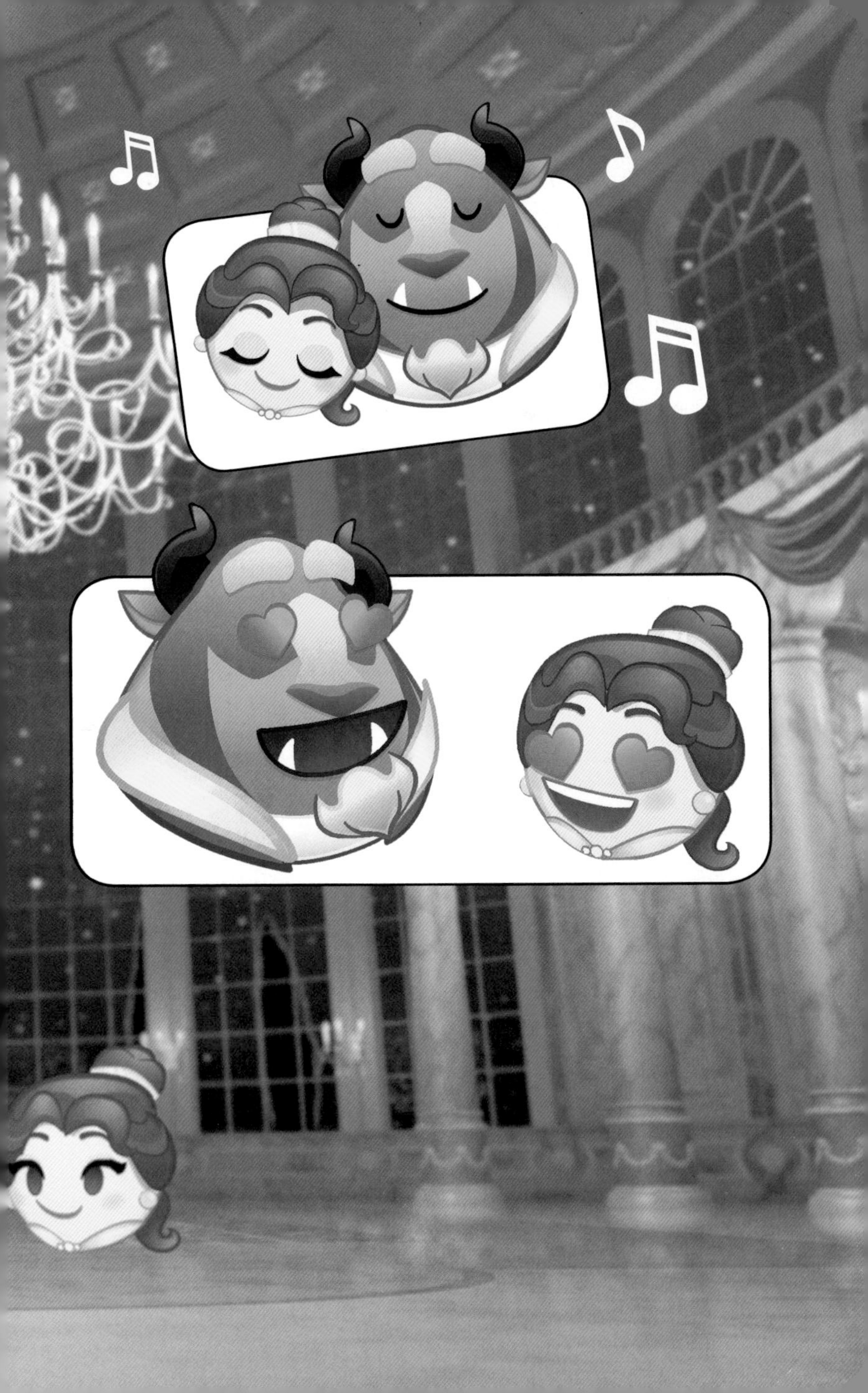

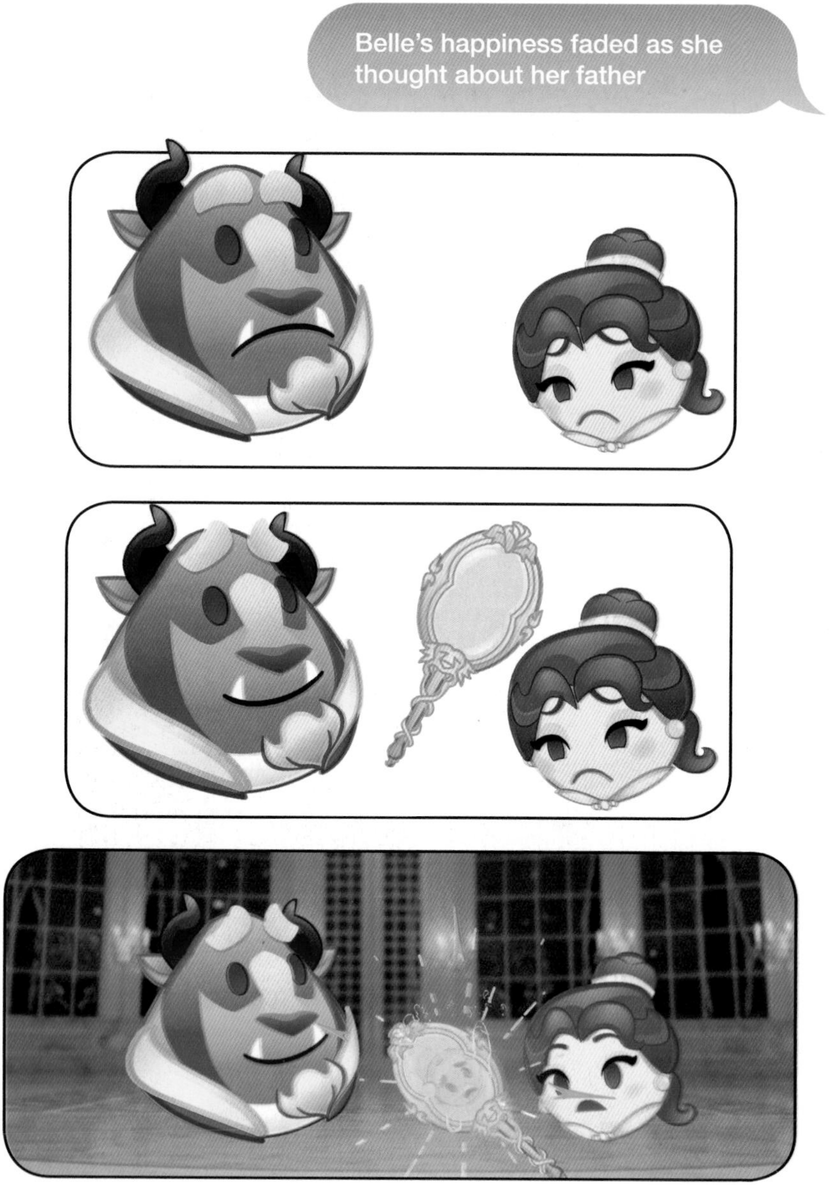
Belle's happiness faded as she thought about her father

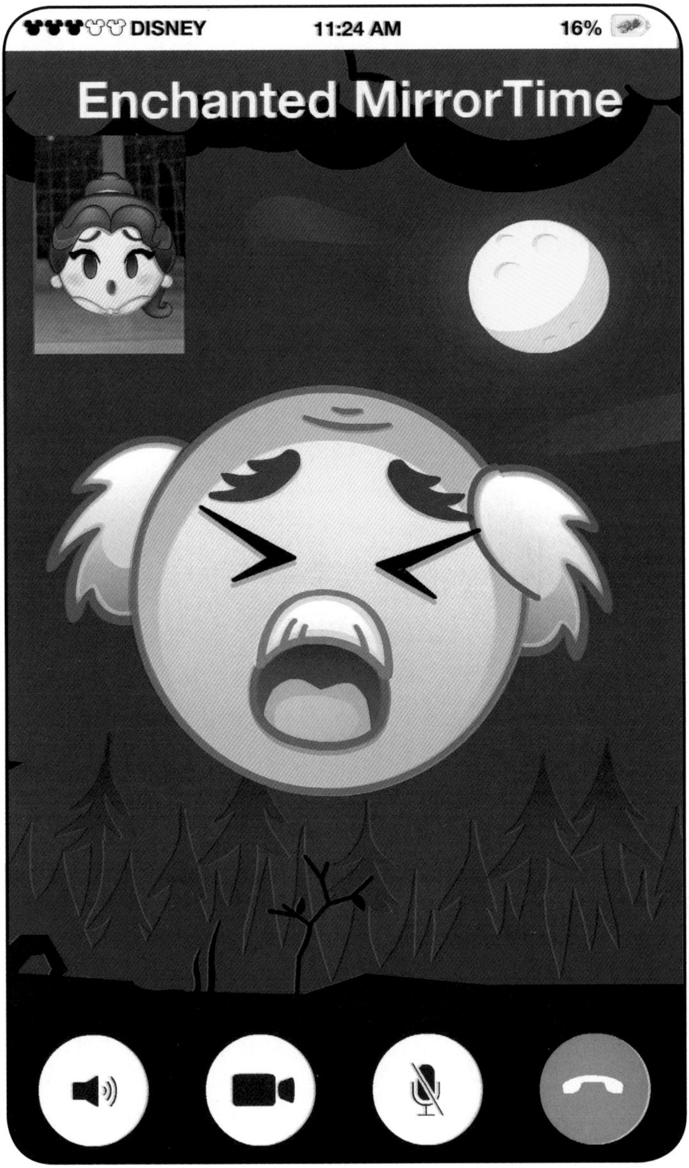
DISNEY
11:24 AM
16%
Enchanted MirrorTime

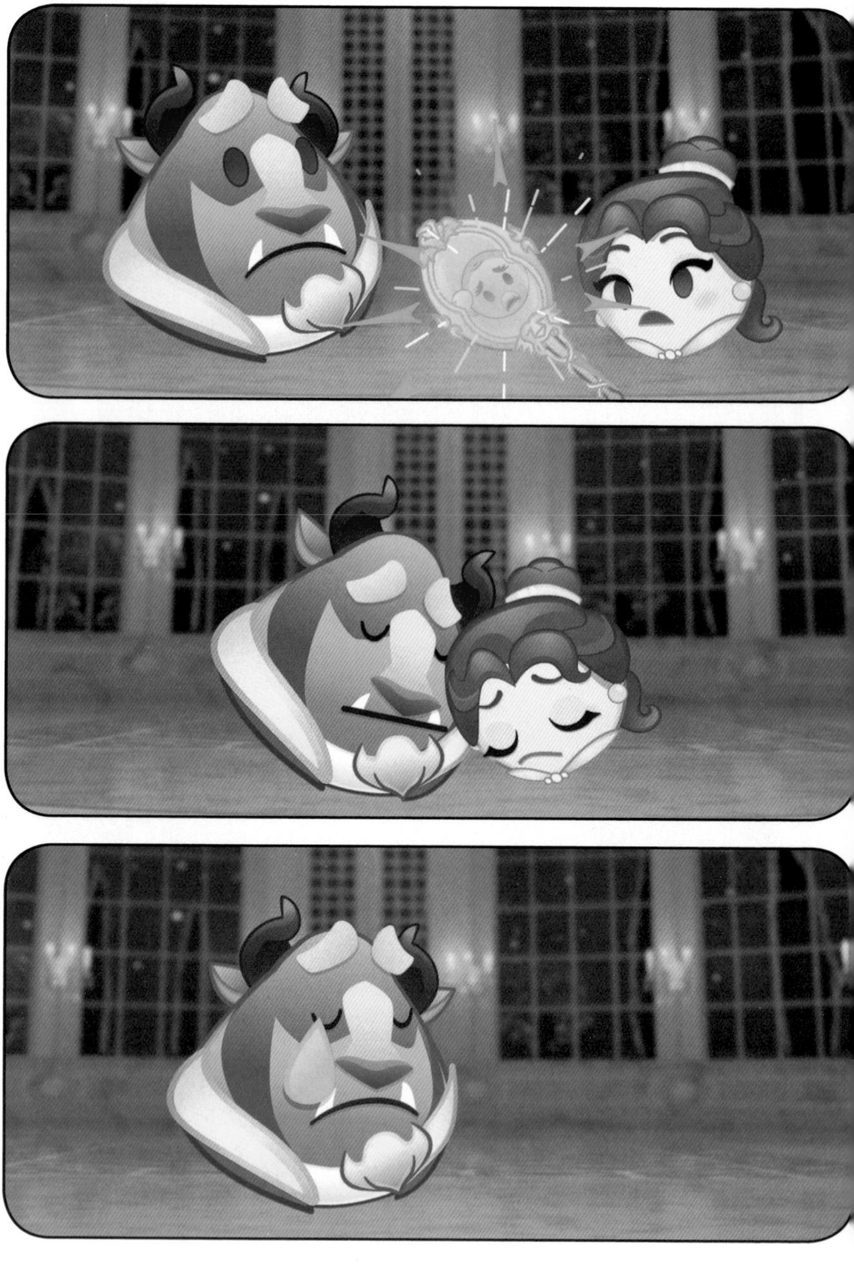

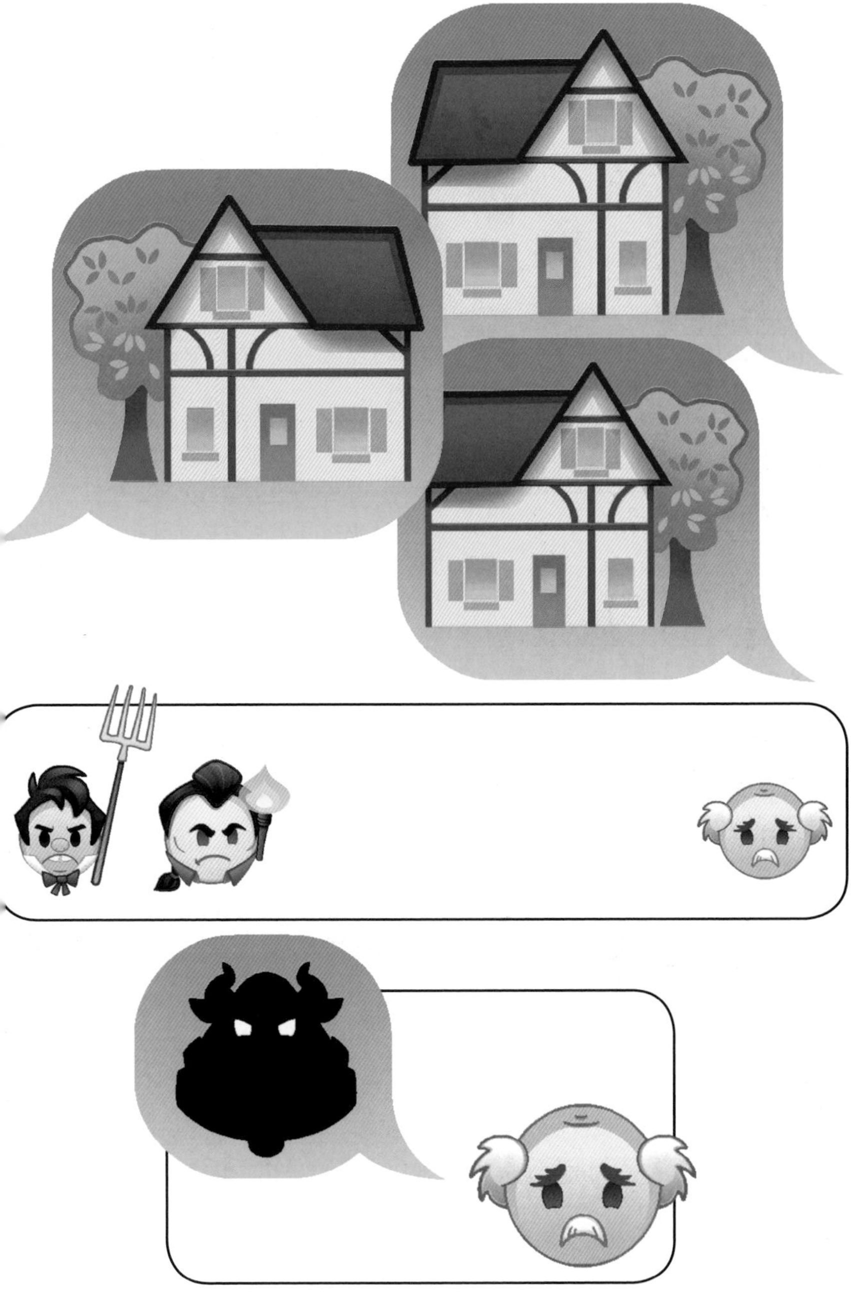

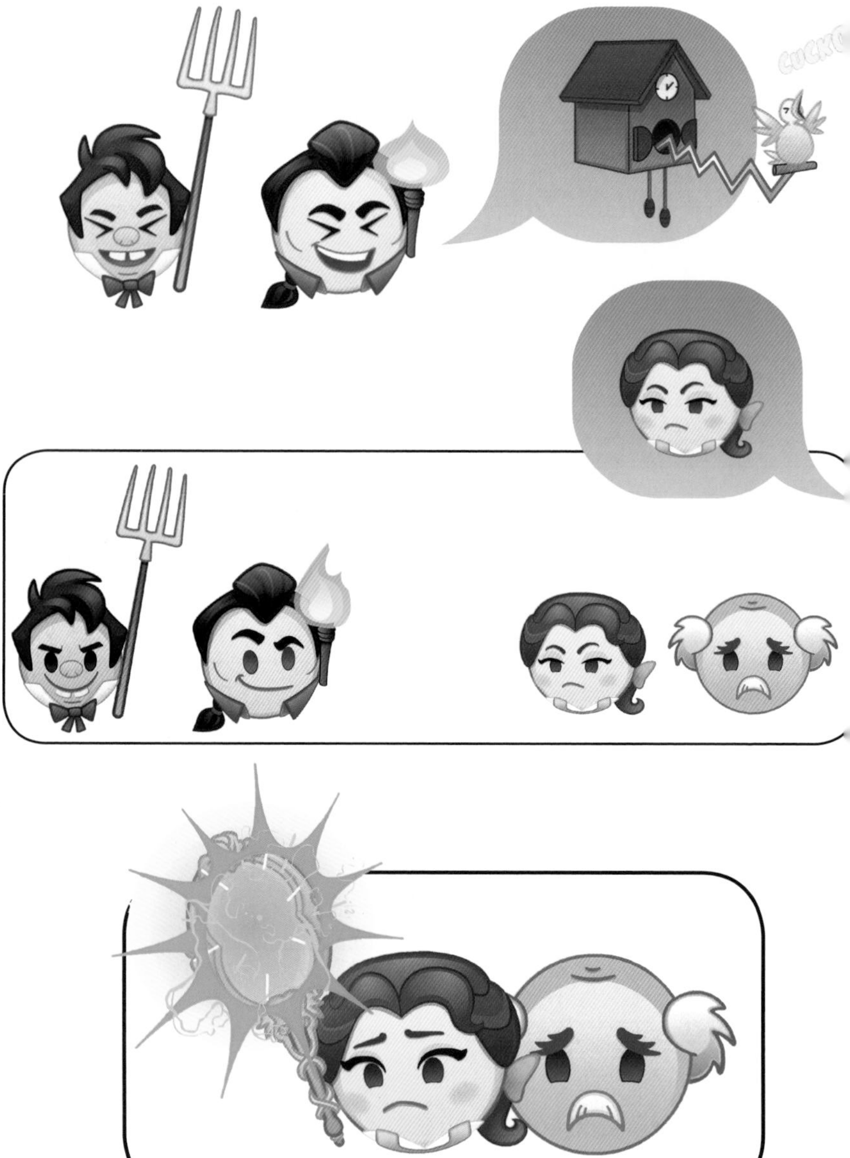

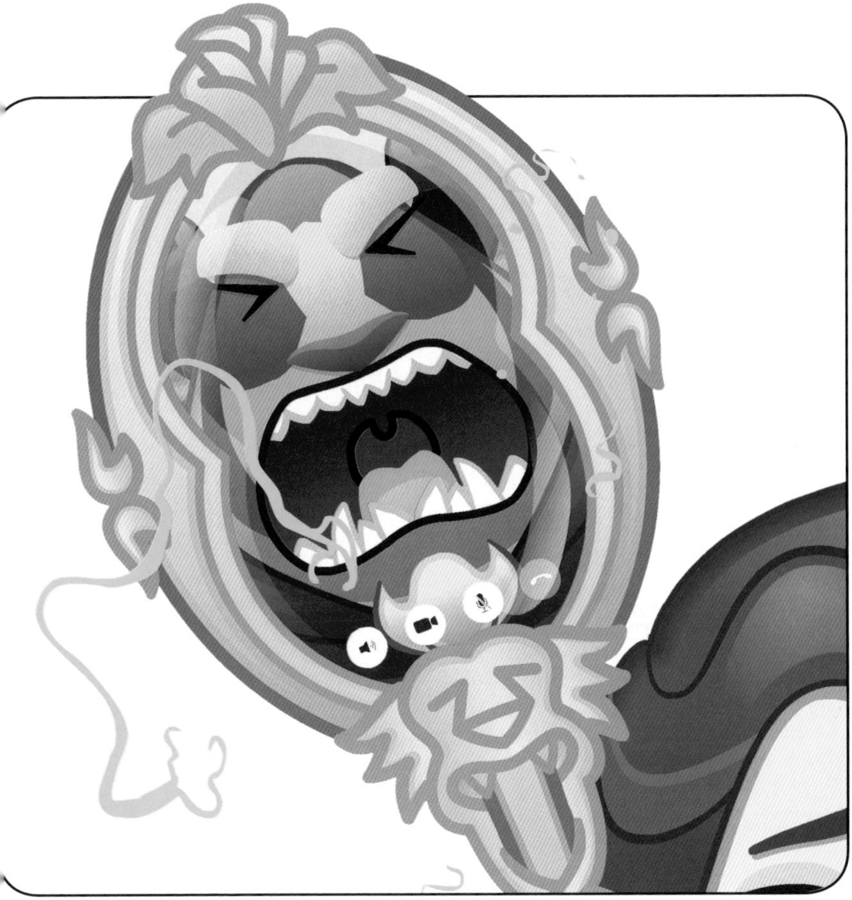

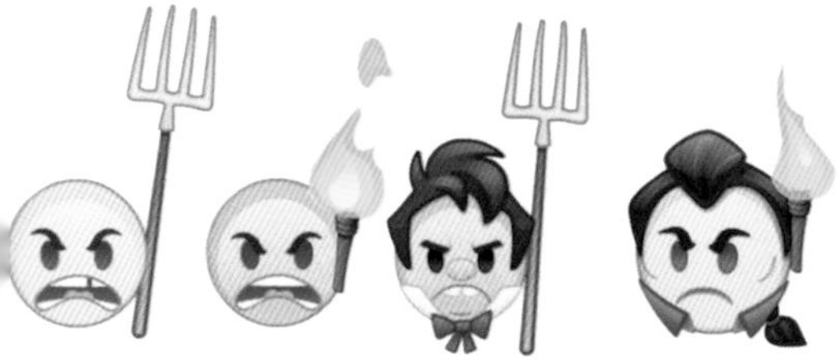

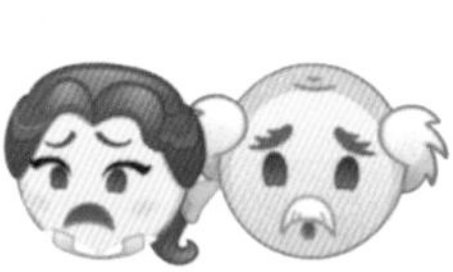

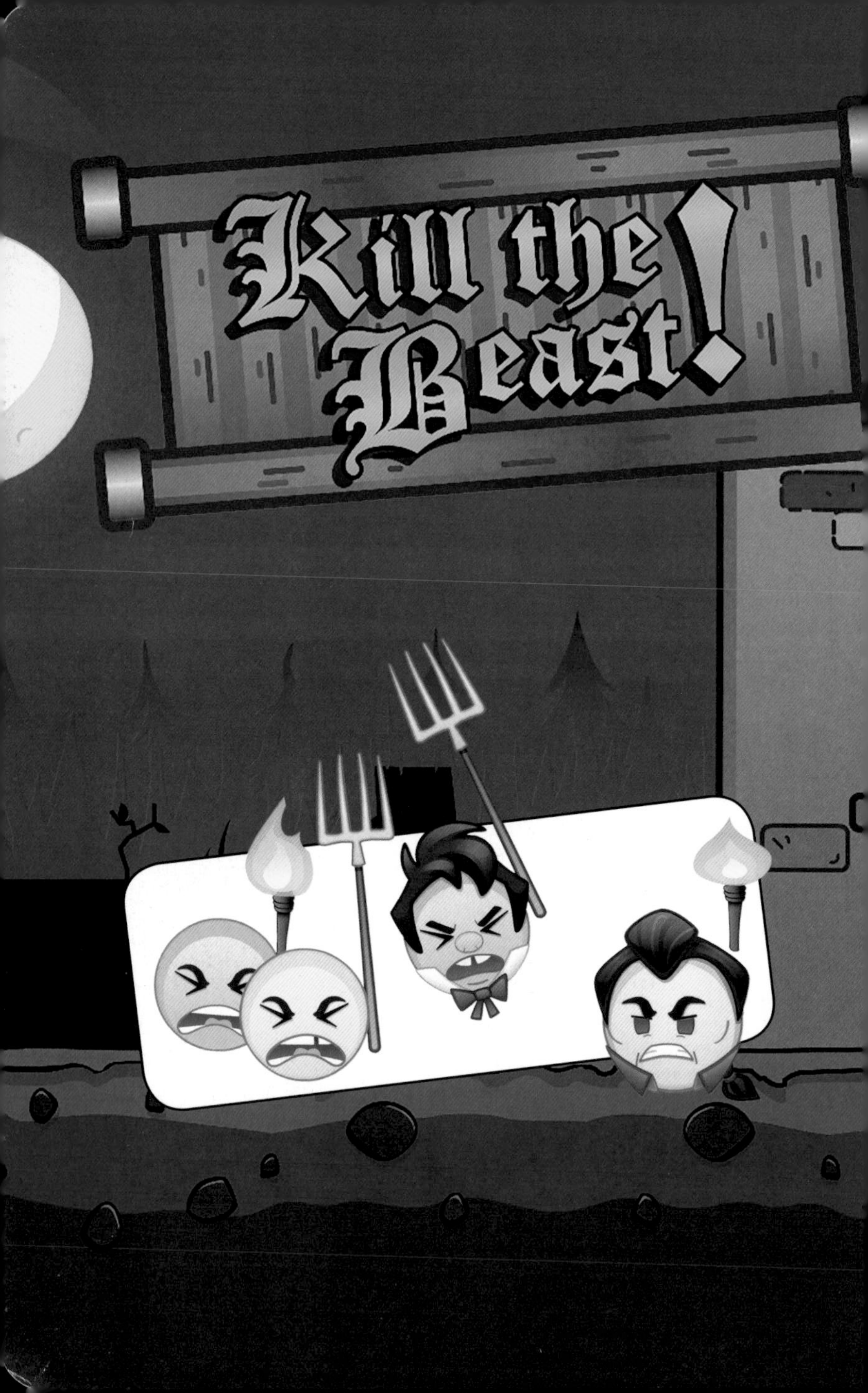
Kill the Beast!

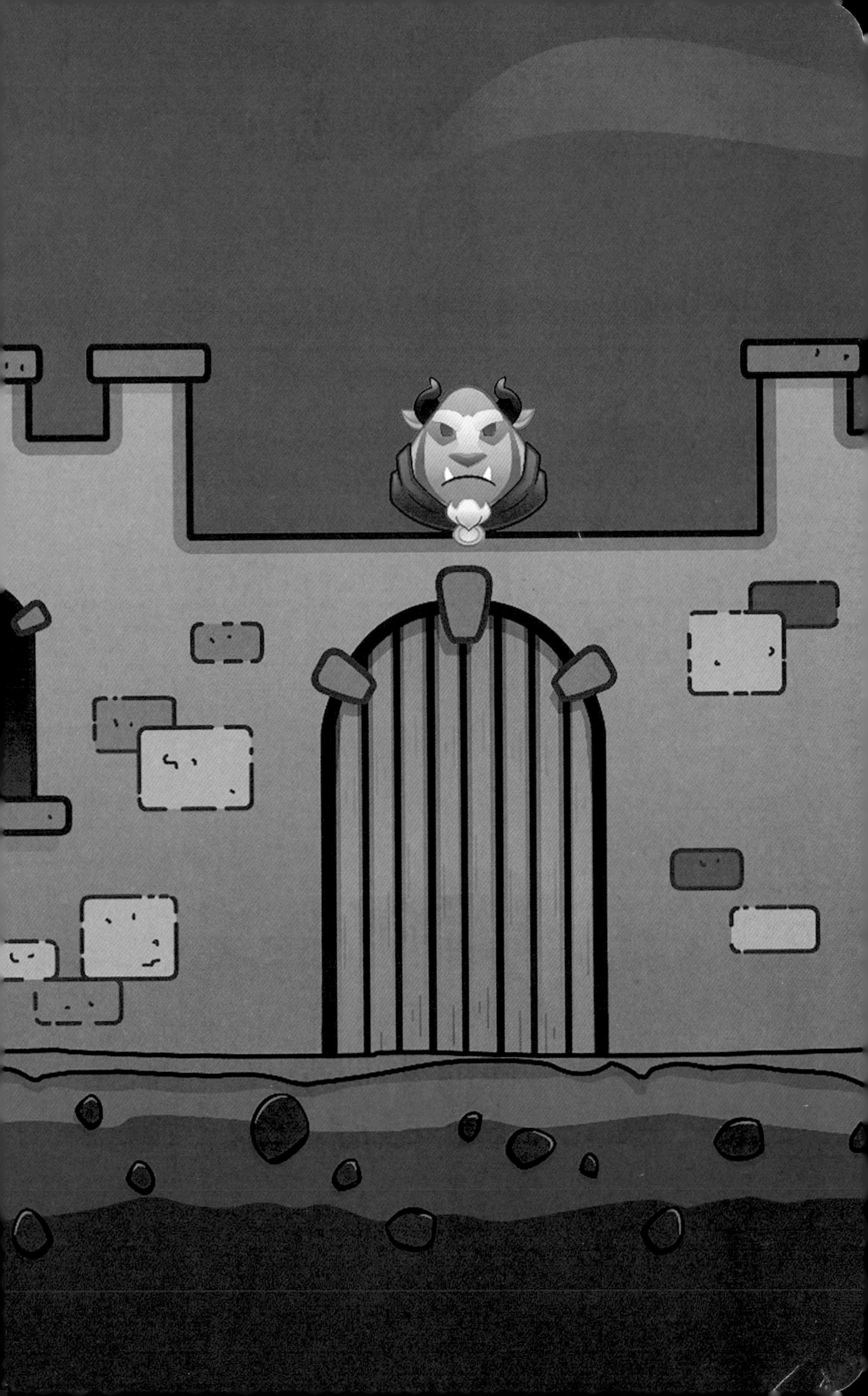

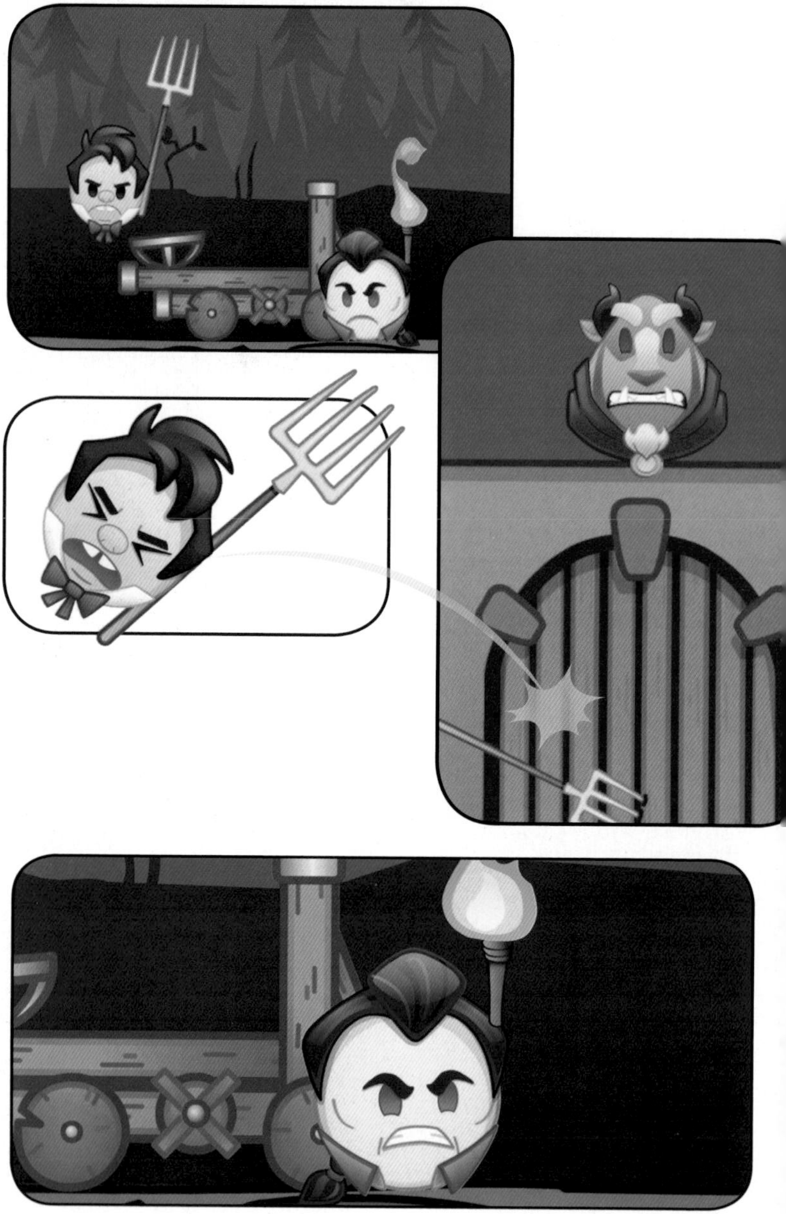

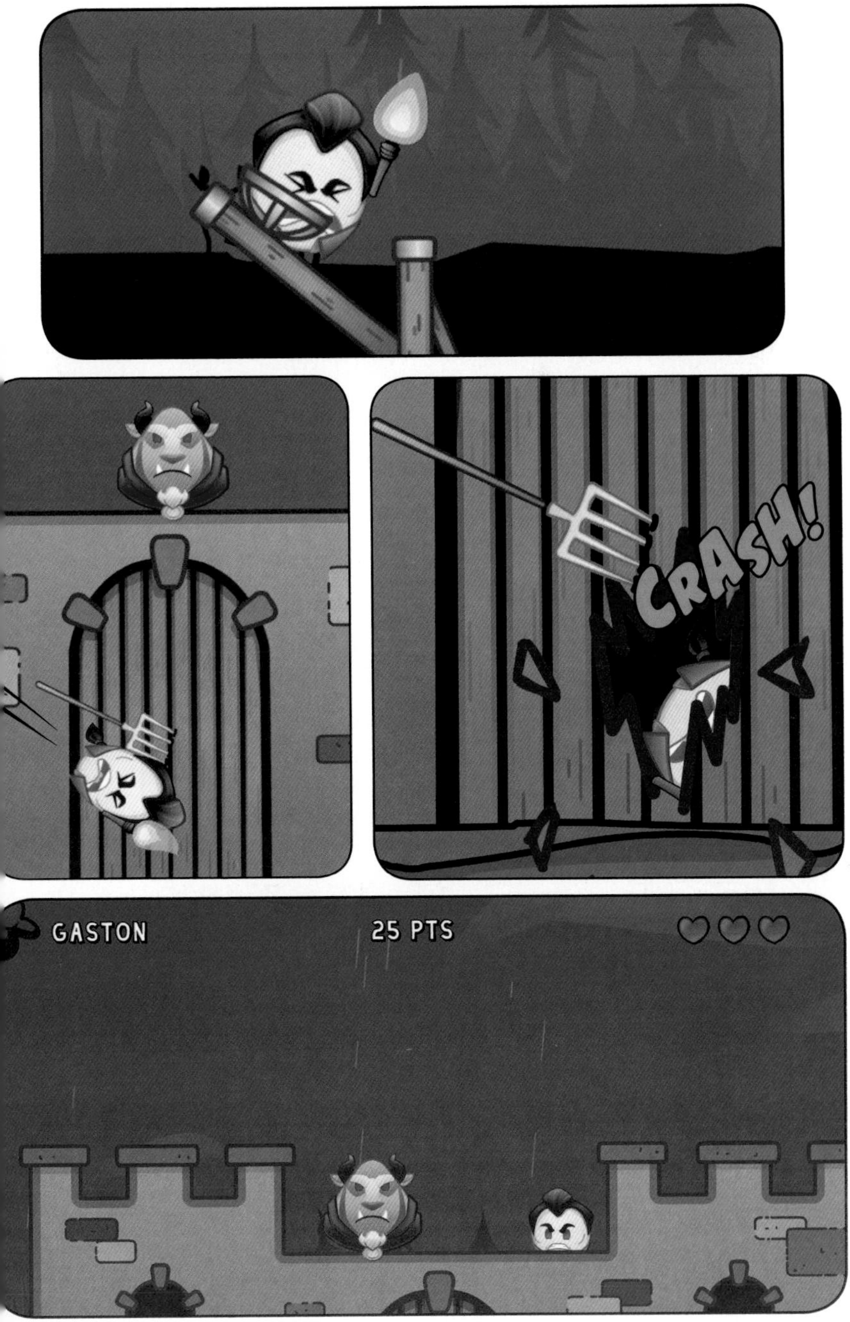
CRASH!
GASTON
25 PTS

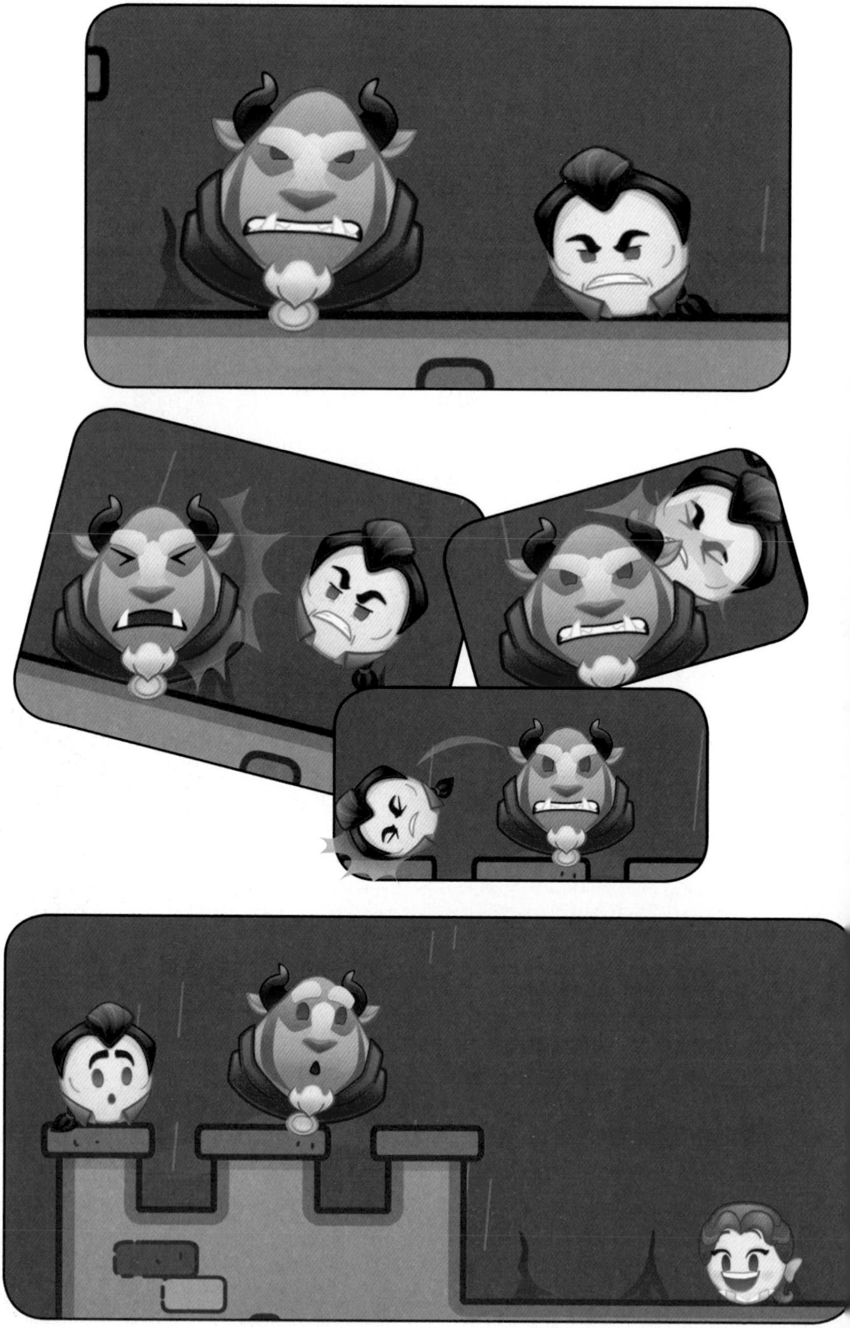

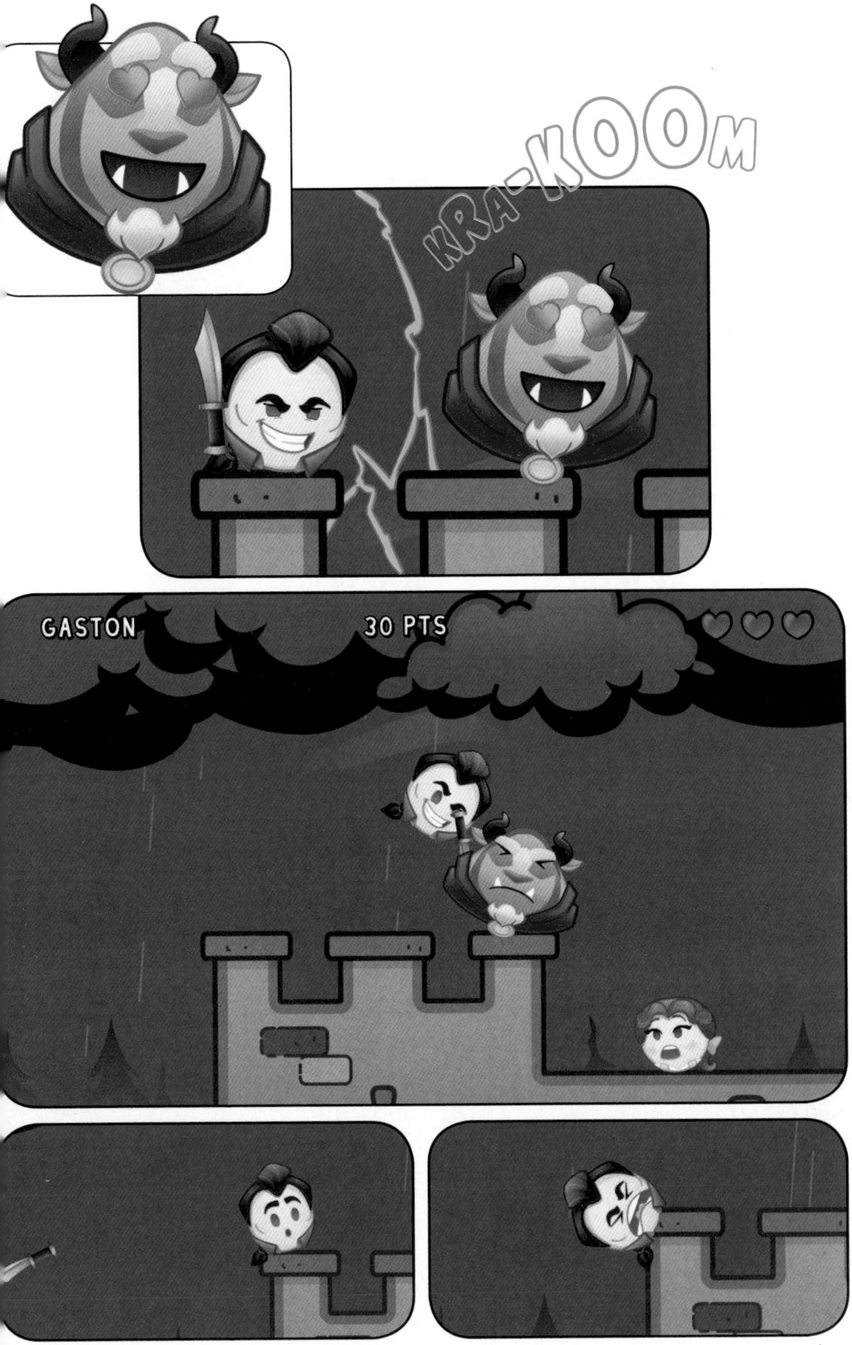
KRA-KOOM
GASTON
30 PTS

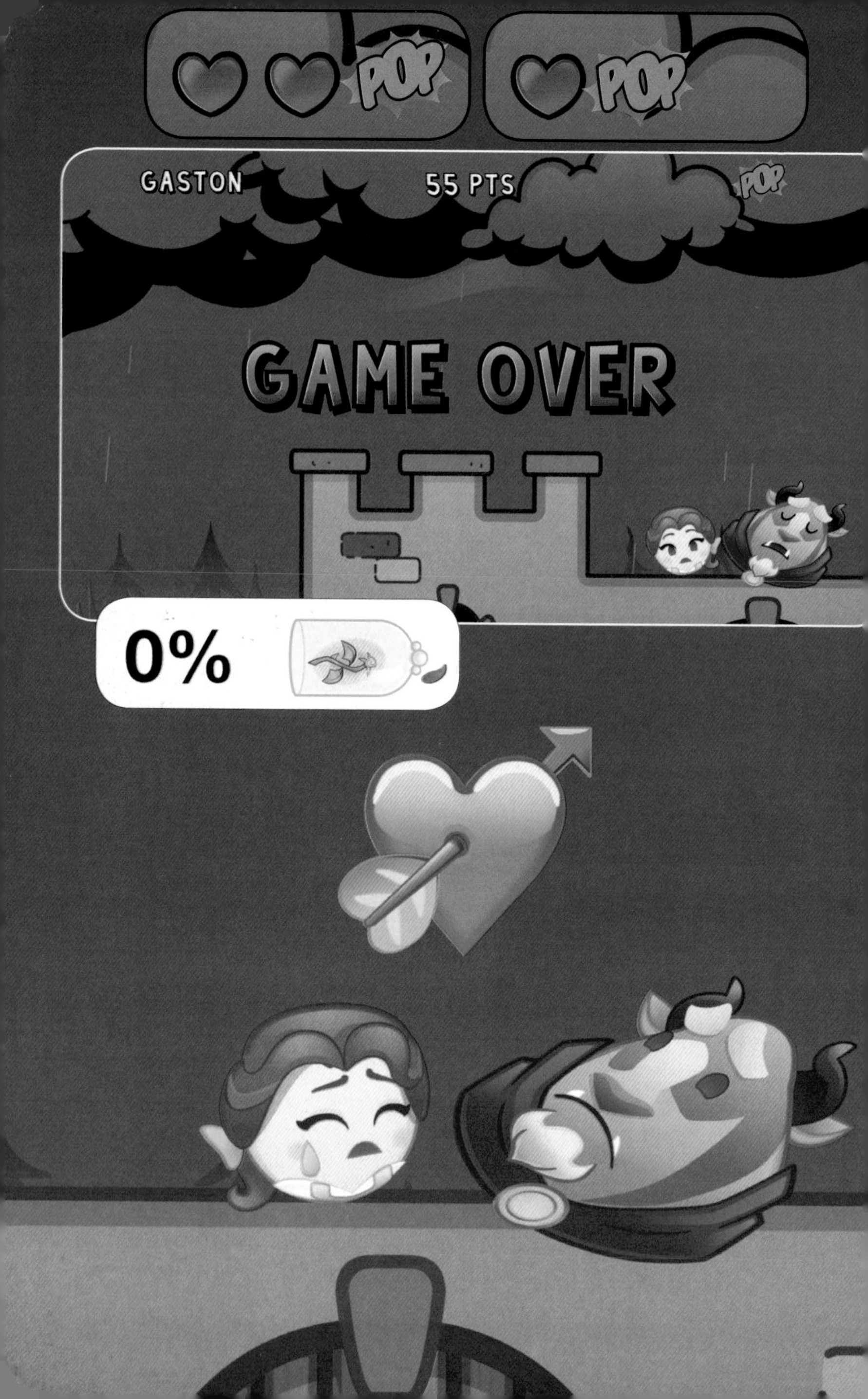
POP
POP
GASTON
55 PTS
POP
GAME OVER
0%

UPDATING OS
BEAST

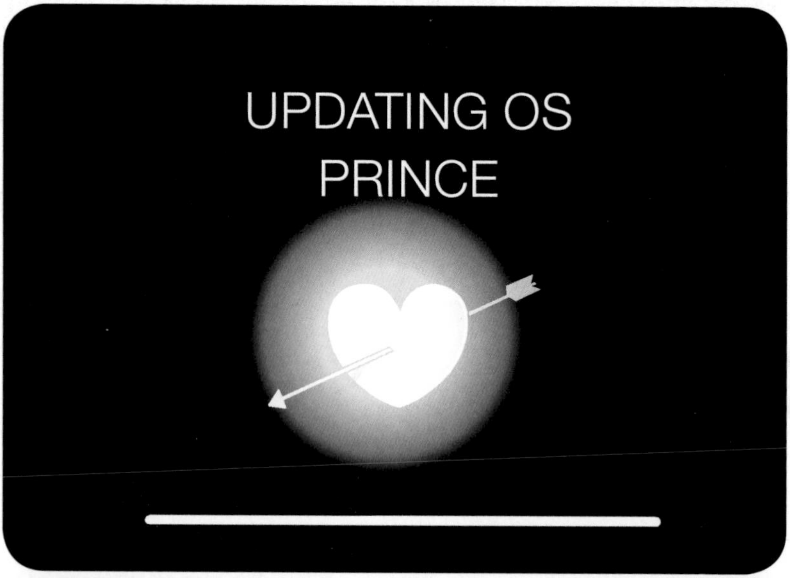
UPDATING OS
PRINCE

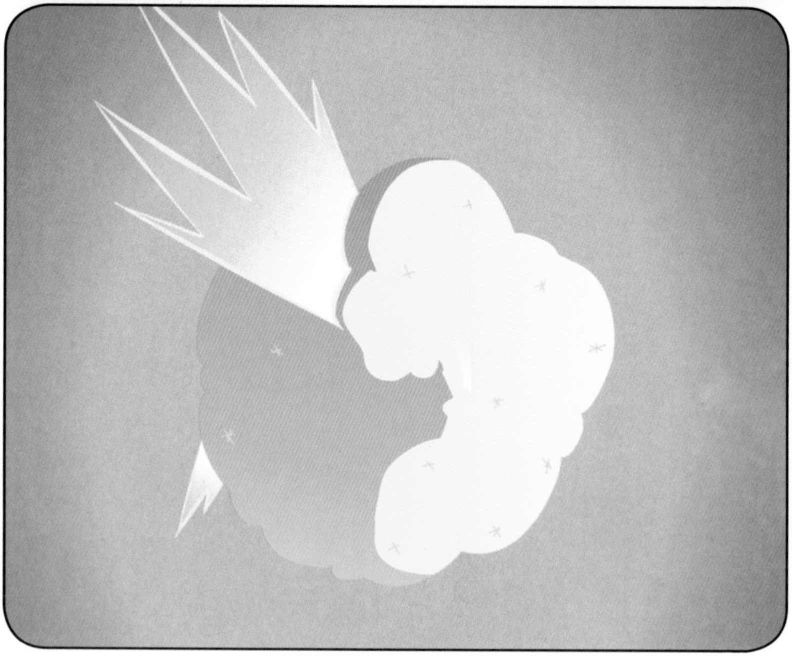

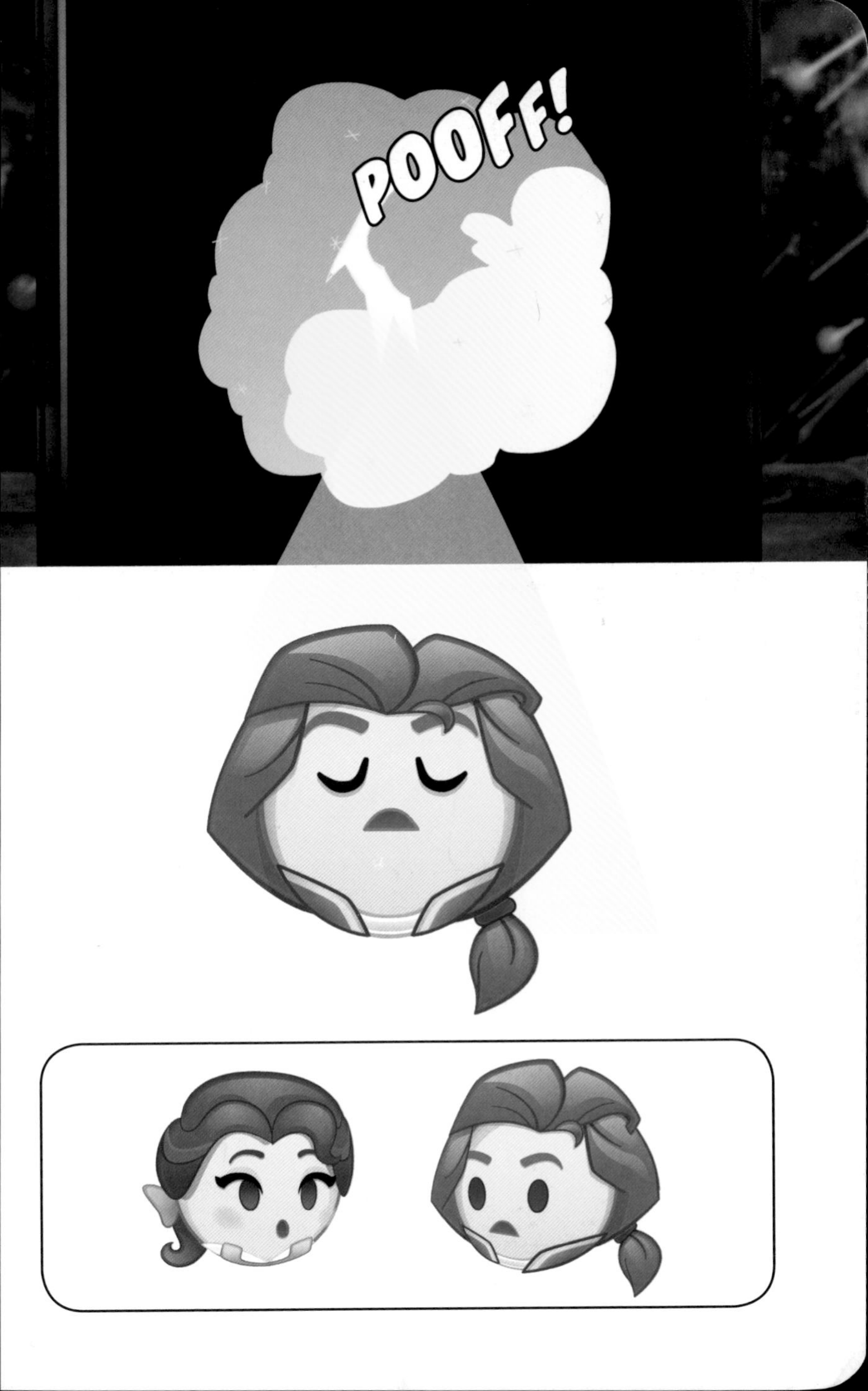
POOFF!

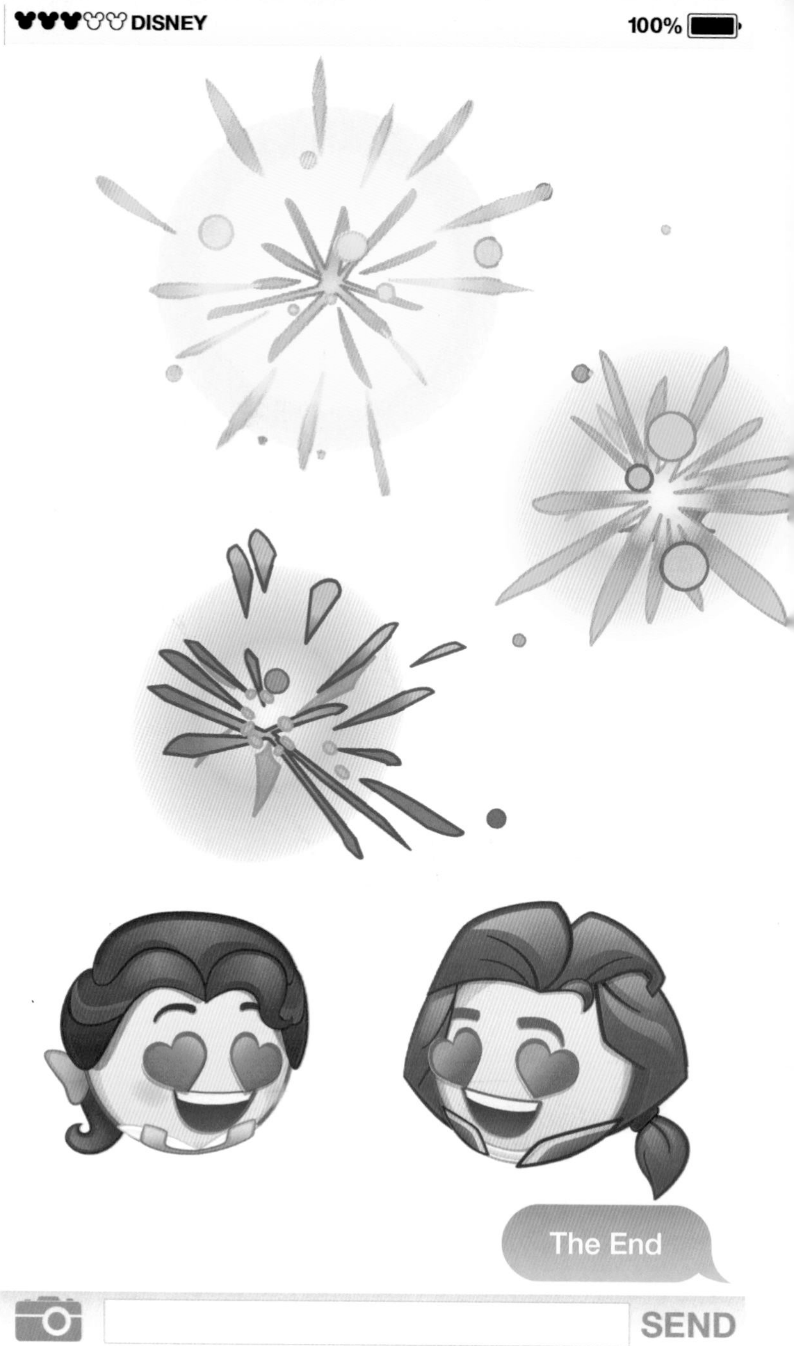
DISNEY
100%
The End
SEND

Belle

Belle is an intelligent girl from a small ▮▮ village. An avid reader,  dreams of adventures "in the great wide somewhere," like those in her beloved 📖.

With her spirit and intelligence,  sees beyond appearances and does what it takes to turn her dreams into reality.

Beast

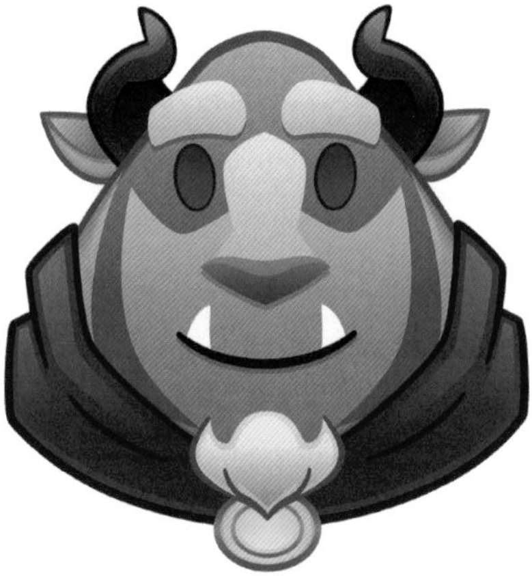

Once an arrogant prince, the Beast and his  were cursed by an 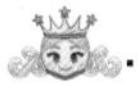.

, and his castle filled with enchanted objects, are waiting for a girl to break the spell.

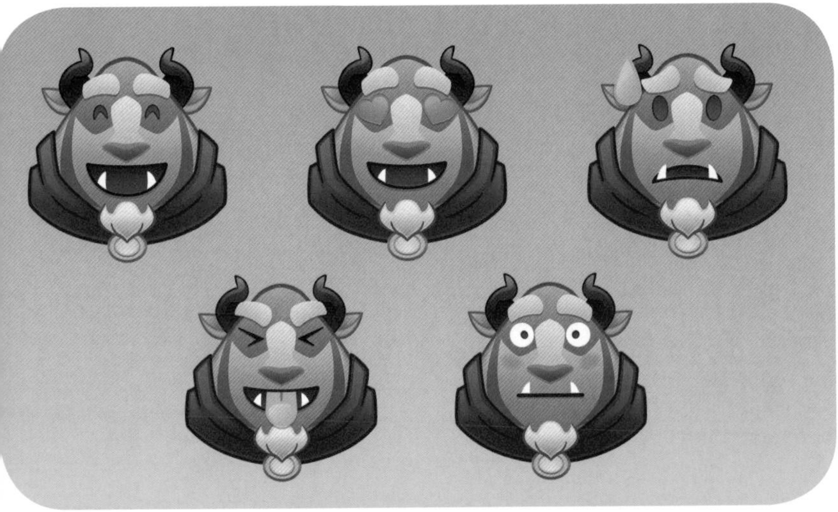

Gaston is an egotistical hunter who vies for 's hand in marriage and is determined not to let anyone else win her 🖤.

Maurice

Maurice is an eccentric inventor and 's loving father.
When he gets lost and ends up a prisoner in 🐺's castle, 👩
must exchange her freedom for his.

Collect them all!

As Told By

Disney emoji

CINESTORY
COMIC

CINESTORY
COMIC

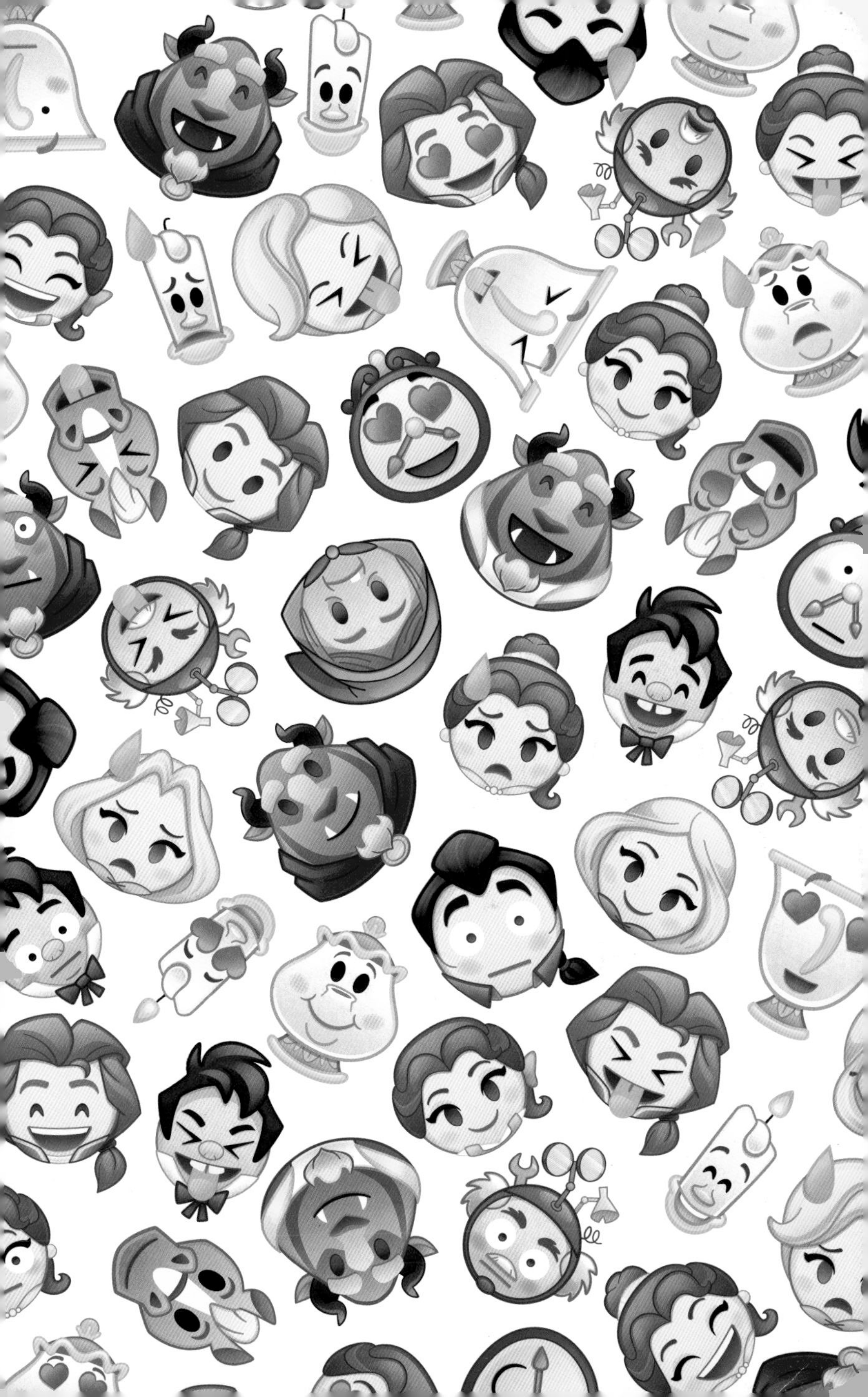

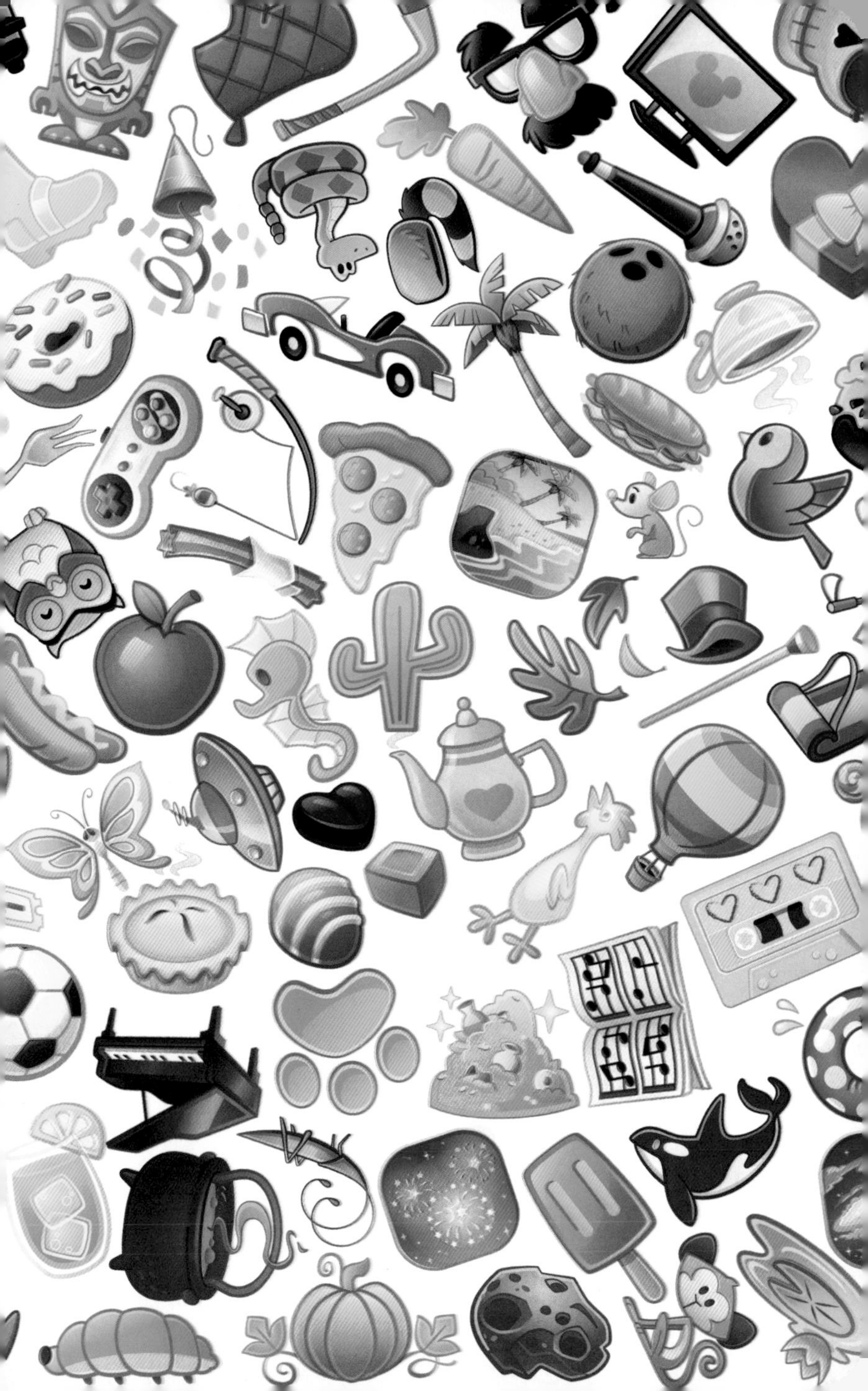

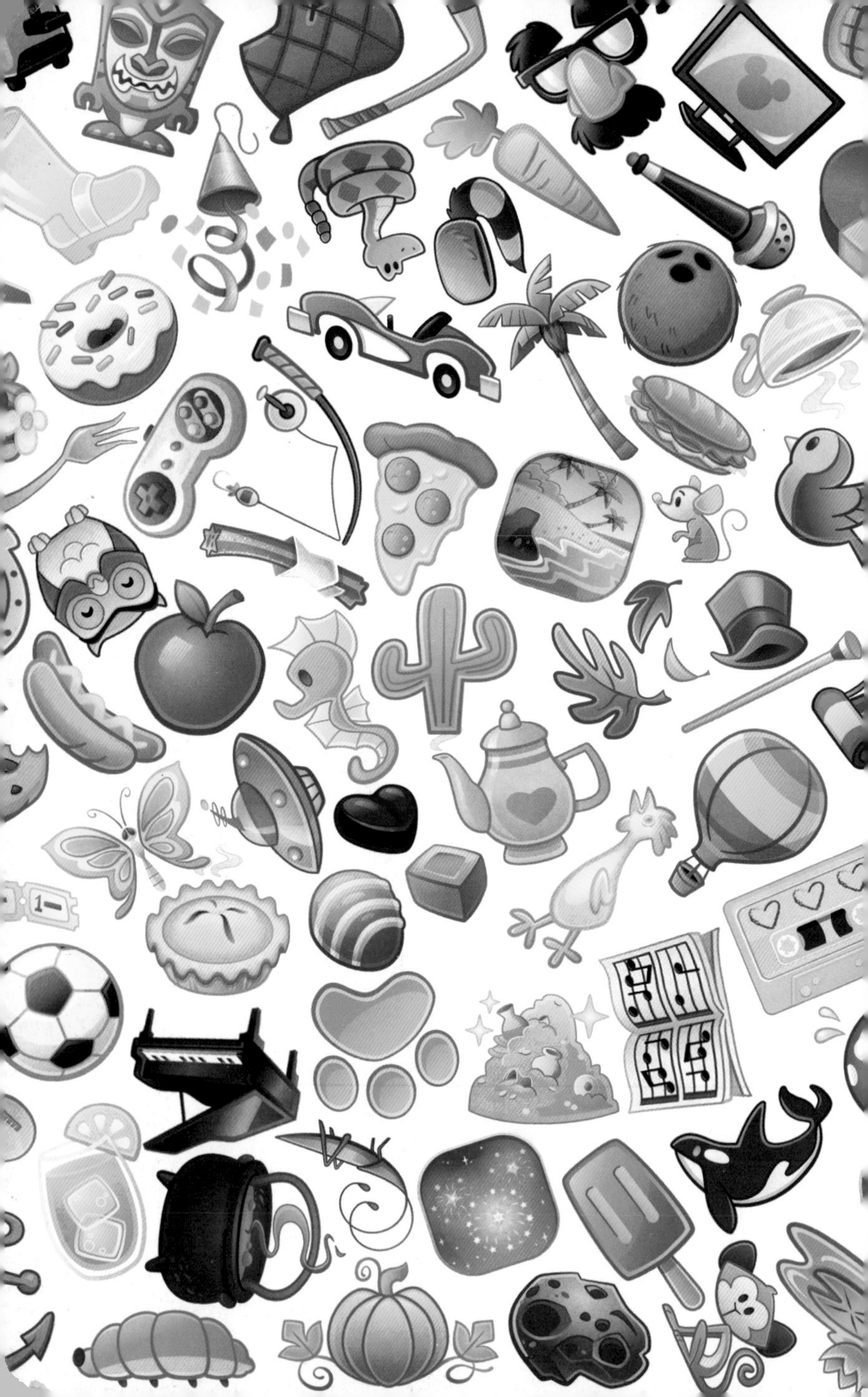